THROUGH THE GRANITE MIRROR

Through the Granite Mirror

Pauline Sheppard

UNITED WRITERS
Cornwall

UNITED WRITERS PUBLICATIONS LTD
Ailsa, Castle Gate, Penzance, Cornwall.
www.unitedwriters.co.uk

British Library Cataloguing in Publication Data:
A catalogue record for this book is
available from the British Library.

ISBN 9781852001964

Printed and bound in Great Britain by
United Writers Publications Ltd.,
Cornwall.

Dedicated to

The Cornish Hedges

Secrets & Lies – i

The Past was wrapped in sacking and laid gently between the first two rows of stone above the grounders in the middle section of Dry Field hedge. The sacking was covered with earth and tamped down before the next two rows of stone and rab, and the following two, until finally the turf was laid across the top. A secret was safe, and a promise kept.

The Return

It smelled of fox. A sharp feral scent of dusk and dawn. The grass still sparkled with dew. He walked briskly. He wasn't thinking about his surroundings, only his destination. He jumped the stone stile, landed badly and swore aloud: "Bastard bleddy hell!" A claxon of crows flapped into the air, then dropped back between the stalks of daffodils to continue feeding. He sat still and stared up towards the copse. There was no longer a little tin hut in the trees, but he knew that. It had gone in his childhood; along with his ability to jump the granite stiles. He felt in his pocket for the envelope, to remind himself of what had brought him back to Cornwall.

Two Letters

A letter had come from Billy Blewett's Aunty Rose. Billy's Aunty Rose had been like an aunty to all Billy's friends, his real friends, which were a select few.

The letter said: "Dear Benjamin, My lovely nephew Billy has died after a short illness. We're having a funeral Thursday week over Towednack. Billy wanted to be buried there, close to his father. I do hope you can come. Billy always talked about you. In fact he has left you this letter which I do here enclose. Yours sincerely, Rose Blewett."

The enclosed said: 'tO sTanDbaCK' in Billy's very individual handwriting, a random mixture of upper and lower case characters. He'd learned some basics at Primary School and had considered the basics to be enough for written communication for the rest of his life. Billy was a practical man. Inside the envelope there was a Christmas card which said, "To my nephew Billy, Happy Christmas from Aunty Rose." On the back of the card was Billy's message:

'sTanDbAcK yOu baSTarD yOud beTteR cOMe hOmE fOr MY fuNral. IvE LeFt YOu mY fErReTs. THeyre gOodunns. yOull fiNd uN In teh usuLe pLaace. DuN LEavEn tOo lonG mIne. iLeFt'n wiTh DRy fOOd. TEs LiKe CRack To a FeRreT. yOurS biLl.'

There was also a ten pound note. 'P.s. aVe 1 oN Me' it said.

The Return

He stuffed the letters back into his pocket, then stood up gingerly and tested his weight. Stomping gently he began to shuffle round on the spot, taking in the surrounding view like a lighthouse beam; as they used to do when they were children, out on the spit of rock down River Cove. It had seemed so high and dangerous to the boys when they were seven years old and looking for mussels. He took a 360 degree turn to look from the right of the copse, out and down the incline until the sea and sky became joined in the mist-rising morning. Then round to landward, from where he had come. There was Penzance in the distance, and Mounts Bay with St. Michael's Mount a black cut-out against the mist-silvery sky. He continued his turn, looking back towards the copse and across the tiny fields and the granite hedges with their yellow crowns of gorse and jagged blackthorn. Beyond the copse, nestled in the next valley, was Trevarnon farmhouse, but that had gone too. The house was still there but no longer was it a farmhouse, though the fields still spread a patchwork carpet out towards the cliffs and the Land's End.

It all smelled the same, it was the same musty, mossy, damp coconut-salty country that he remembered; but it wasn't the same. Fifteen years ago he'd walked down from the copse to catch a bus to the station in Penzance and left Cornwall for good. This morning he'd left for good again. Had he not met John Matthews outside the station, he would be on his way to Plymouth by now. But he had met John Matthews and nothing could change that. There was nothing to do but to stank on, while his inner voice sang out, "I shouldn't be here! I should be on the Bristol train."

From the Top of the Hill

The copse was smaller than he remembered. It still gave shelter from the south-westerlies though. As soon as he entered the thicket of stunted sycamore, blackthorn and gorse, the air became quiet. He walked the badger trail with his feet as his body pushed through the tangle of die-back bramble and bracken until he came to the pancake rocks of granite. He scrambled over the rocks to the highest point and stared out over the little fields, criss-crossed by the granite hedges. He knew them all: Black Down, Stony Ground, The Hump, Fuggy Du, Sanctuary, The Meadow, Daffodil, Longfield and Dry Field. It was his land, the land of his father and his father before that. Trevarnon Farm was flanked on the right by Mr and Mrs Blewett's up the Carn, and Harry Trengrouse's farm over Chy Tolver on the left. A river came down through the land into River Cove. The boundary line between Trevarnon and Carn Farm ran invisibly down the centre of the river. At the cliff edge the hedges were rougher, coffin-stoned hedges built from a series of granite boulders; and the blackthorn pointed landwards, waves of salty black twigs with foaming crests of white blossom in springtime. In his day there would have been sheep up by the copse, cows in the lower fields, a few pig arcs in Sanctuary, and winter wheat, caulis or spuds elsewhere. These days the land was contracted out. This season was daffodils. Pickers moved like ants between the rows of flowers.

He was about to jump down from the rocks but thought better of it and made his way down slowly. He went to where the little green tin hut used to stand and sat down on the ground to think. Jack Dash had built the hut. At the end of the war Grandad had pulled down the old corrugated lean-to on the back of the barn to make it easier to turn his new tractor and trailer in the yard. Jack had asked if he could build a shack from the best of the tin and timbers. His hut was no bigger than a wagon. Jack set it up on blocks, timber-framed and tin-clad. He painted it green so that it melded into the trees of the copse. Inside he lined his hut with wood. It had a little cast-iron stove at one end and a bed at the other. Jack built shelves, a cupboard, and made a table and two chairs. It was lit by a paraffin lamp; he had a wash jug and bowl for washing, and he collected water from the well, just as they used to do in the farmhouse until the 1950s.

He stared out over the cliffs to the Atlantic. He'd loved visiting the little tin hut and listening to Jack's stories about his home in Poland. As a boy he had sat on the wooden step of the tin hut to watch the big ships sail far away into the horizon.

11

Today he could just make out the line of a tanker. Looking away into the sea-sky distance had always made him feel a deep sense of belonging to be on the north Cornish coast. He didn't want to be here but he couldn't belong anywhere else. He stared at the ground, all too aware of the farmhouse and the meadow behind a hedge of hawthorn which sheltered the little orchard on the cliff side. Closer still to the cliffs, on the far side of the farmhouse, was Dry Field, where his brother Eddie was waiting. It was fifteen years since he'd last seen the farmhouse, and his brother. He shivered in the early morning air as fingers of sea mist drifted in over the cliffs to hover in corners, and the world became timeless, as had the long hours he had spent back in the late 1980s, when he'd run away from the farmhouse to work in the meadow.

The Meadow

"There's a philosophy an' a practicality to a trade like hedging." He'd heard the old men say that and they were right. He'd laughed at first when his father told him, "You've got to listen to the stones." But his father had been right too. His own knowing had come in the meadow, and long after the cows had gone. His father had been dying then and the world was changing; but even though there were no beasts to eat the grass, and the brambles were crawling across the good Cornish grassland because there were no beasts to crop it, he'd still found a pleasure, and a comfort, in maintaining the old meadow hedges.

The farmhouse was within calling distance, should he be needed. It was little more than a hundred yards away on the other side of a group of overgrown sycamores, a Lilac tree his mother had planted, and the remains of a dug-out he and his brother had constructed when they were boys. But that divide was enough to create two worlds. He'd felt angry in the dying house, but out in the meadow it was peaceful and calm. He'd laboured in the autumn to keep the brambles in check and rebuilt the stone hedges set by his grandfather and the ancestors. He'd always loved to work alone. To feel the wind on his face, to hear the birds, not just the singing. He loved to hear the wings skirring as birds flew into the blackthorn thickets to roost. He loved to be at one with the hedge and its world. When he stopped for crowst, for the dark red tea-leafed tea and a pasty, he would lean his back upon the stones and close his eyes. Then, while listening to the hedge speaking; to the rustling of lizards, beetles, the infinite life around him, he was full to bursting. No other job gave him such life.

"Take time to learn that," his father had said. "There's a right way an' a wrong way, an' everyone have his own way. What other job give you that?" No other job had ever given him such fulfilment. With the stones singing in the open country he felt at one with himself. It filled his spirit with a life force that he carried back into the dying house. It seemed to him that his father was the last in a line who had worked the land the same way for centuries. Men who had somehow become part of the ground they'd tamed and trodden.

The Fox in the Meadow

He'd hunkered into the dark side of the hedge as the sun set pink streaks behind him. He would have to go back to the house soon, but not yet.

It was the best time of night, dusk ... the stones nearly gone quiet, just sitting with the hedge. He was not alone, he became

13

aware of sharing his space. Out from the bracken came a fox. It sat close by; so close he could smell the musty scent of its fur. It was an old dog fox. It'd been around some, and the eyes which stared back at him seemed somehow deep with old knowing. Unafraid, his companion lifted a rear leg, pissed against the hedge, and proceeded to scratch itself. Then it turned away and picked a blackberry with great delicacy and ownership. Its nose titched up at the end, then its lip curled back as it nipped off the fruit with its front teeth. It was sweet to its taste and it nosed around for more berries. "Thass right, boy," he thought. "You enjoy that. Thass yours, that is."

He marvelled how the fox could nose through the brambles without getting scratched or tangled in the thorns as he would have done. Yes, the berries were set just right for a fox, low in the field. He was glad he'd cut them well back last year for them to grow like that ... he'd cut them by hand, the old way, the way Grandad and Jack Dash had done, with the hook. As a result the brambles were fresh and young. There was a whole crop of them, at a really good height for a fox. They sat together for what might have been five or fifteen minutes, or much longer. Time stood still as he sat and the old fox nosed and picked its way through the brambles. Then the fox raised its head and scented the air, before looking back at him as if to say, "I'm off now, pard," and it sprang up onto the hedge to disappear in the night blackness.

He remained, sitting alone, until it was truly dark, wanting to stay in the life of the hedge for as long as was possible. He brushed the hair from his forehead and noticed the taste of earth on his hand. "You got to love the country you're workin' with. You got to be part of it, taste it. Thass what I think," said his father's voice.

Much later he crossed towards the farmhouse feeling

14

satisfied; and the feeling of dread that always came upon him as he opened the kitchen door didn't happen.

That was the night his father had died.

The Hosken Boys – i

As he left the copse behind him, he could see across Longfield to Dry Field. There were pickers in Longfield, a lot of them. He could see the old hedge in Dry Field. Several sections showed damage, probably caused by rabbits. In the centre of the old hedge there was a large gap, about ten foot he thought, where someone had collapsed the stones and piled them nearby, ready to effect a repair. "You can't work the end til you have the middle," Grandad had said that, so had Jack, and Father. "If you want a hedge mended or built, you get the Hosken Boys." Folk'd always said that, and it had been true. Until the Hosken Boys found out they couldn't work together any longer.

It wasn't too late, he could turn around and go back to the station. It wasn't healthy to walk into the past. That's why he'd stayed away, so that he might bury the past. He'd only come back to Cornwall for Billy Blewett's funeral; and now John Matthews had told him Eddie was working back on the farm.

Hoskens had worked the land at Trevarnon for 400 years. The Hoskens had farmed for generations. There'd been nothing unusual about that when he was growing up. He was a farmer's son, like his father, and his grandfather before. It was who he was, or at least, it was who he had been, up until 1993.

He decided to go the long way to Dry Field. He decided to walk down to Trevarnon, take a look at the old house, and maybe the meadow too. He smiled. His brother Eddie would be mad as hell by the time he got to Dry Field.

Hidden in Full View

The Cornish hedges are lines in the landscape. Like the stitching on a tapestry they are looked at without being seen. Hundreds of visitors stop their cars in the lay-by on craggy Rosewall Hill. They take pictures of the view out towards the Carracks, Seal Island. You would be hard pressed to take a photograph of any part of the Cornish landscape which did not contain a hedge. The hedges are so familiar to the eye that they are unseen, even when stared at in the photograph album. They are just there, and they have been 'just there' for thousands of years. The most ancient hedges are further to the tip of the peninsula, at the Land's end, near St. Just. Built by man's ancestors to shelter man and beast from wind and rain, their purpose remains unchanged. They have sheltered man and beast for over 3000 years. Cameras capture pictures of farms, engine houses, the sea, rolling moorland: and in between these iconic Cornish images are the hedges.

Few who park in the lay-by on Rosewall Hill actually cross the road and take the footpath into the view. Fewer still leave the footpath and venture onto the old drover's road that follows an ancient Cornish hedge to the cliff. Fewer still cross the stile into Home Field, where the cows graze; and no one bothers to turn right; to walk into the brambles and furze and to follow the badger trail over the hedge and into a thicket . . . into Billy Blewett's land.

Billy Blewett was William Blewett's boy from Carn Farm. Billy was not clever if measured by GCSE but if measured by his affinity to the land he held a professorship. As the small farmers sold up or went bankrupt and the enthusiastic emigrants from city life moved in, it was Billy alone who stayed.

He tucked himself down in a triangle of scrub between the hedges and hung on.

None of the new owners thought it was odd to see him cross their fields because Billy made sure that he became their gardener, hedge trimmer and general factotum. The new landowners grew to feel a deep connection with their new country when Billy Blewett sat in their kitchen. Billy drank their posh coffee, ate their carrot cake, and drank their Malt whisky while he showed the TV Producer how to take care of his gun; taught the Financier how to grow leeks or deal with rats. The new landowners' wives made him cakes and retold his stories at parties in town; they felt confident in their new lives in Cornwall, and were proud of their knowledge of local custom and culture in the place which was home for a few weeks of the year.

Different but the Same

He turned into the lane to Trevarnon. The old granite milk-stand was still there. Someone had run concrete down either side of the grass which grew in the middle of the track. The seed rep. and the postman used to grumble about knocking the exhaust on their vans on the tussocky grass. He and Eddie used to go up the centre with the strimmer, but it hadn't helped. He rounded a corner and there before him stood Trevarnon Farmhouse and the yard. The yard was more a sort of courtyard now. The barns and the milking parlour, even the little pig-shed, were all holiday cottages. It seemed too quiet and empty without the beasts of the farm.

The house looked the same but it had a new roof, new window frames and door, new guttering too. For the whole of his life the gutter had leaked just outside the back door. There was no sign of occupancy, no vehicles in the yard, so he walked up to the kitchen window and stared in. The wall between the old kitchen and the cool, whitewashed pantry had been knocked through. His Mother's scrubbed table had gone, as had the tall dresser, and the corner cupboards with all their nick-nacks and Grandad's cups and certificates. It was all granite work-tops, fitted cupboards, and one of the taps he'd seen in magazines that would give instant boiling water. It was like a dream where everything was familiar and yet strangely unreal. He decided to skip going to the meadow. He visited it frequently in his mind where it remained real, unlike the barren tidiness of the farmhouse and yard. He swung round and headed back up the lane.

What Grandad said: *"Tes diff'rant but the same"*

"It all changed after the war when farmers got on tractors." That's what Grandad used to say. *"See, the old road-man, who used to weed around a group of foxgloves on the hedge, an' cut back the corner for the motorist . . . now, he was a gardener. High up in the cab of a four-by-four tractor with the radio on, a man don't see the butterflies gettin' torn to death by the flail. Thass 'cos he idden no gardener. He's in his head, worryin' about his family, how he'll pay the mortgage. Now . . . this 'ere's the thing, 'ere's the paradox . . . That man in the cab, he's juss the same as the Neolithic man who built hedges in the furst place! All he want is to protect his crops an' feed his family. He's diff'rant, but the same, see."*

The Pickers

Eight mud-lagged transit vans stood half on and half off the high grass verge either side of the gate into Longfield. It was chaotic. They looked as though they'd been dropped from the sky rather than parked. The top of a blue Portaloo showed above the blackthorn hedge by the gate. Tyre marked and churned, the mud exploded out of the field through the gateway and onto the road where the tractors had been coming in and out. Sometimes they came to spray the crop, other times with trailers to carry away the crates of flowers.

There had always been pickers but never such an army as this. He reckoned there must be eighty or more in Longfield alone. The wind was south sou'east with a cold bite and there was no cover away from the hedges.

The pickers worked hard; each to his own rhythm, bending to pick the stems deftly, rising to check the length if it was their first time in the field, or taking a quick measure by eye if they'd been at it for some days. As they put an elastic band at top and bottom of the stems, it was automatic to stretch their backs before bending down again over the rows.

Black plastic crates were filling fast at the end of the rows and as they were filled, they were carried to a loading point not far from the field entrance. Sometimes there were bursts of loud chattering, laughter and calls across the rows, but the work continued all the time. It was relentless, arduous, back-breaking and boring. He'd done it himself years before, piece work, seeing who could pick the most caulis, daffs, spuds, who'd get the most money in a day. Making it a sport had been the only thing that had kept him going. There was a fag packet half trodden into the mud, he picked it up. It looked like the writing he'd seen in Uncle Jack's books, Polish, but it was hard to tell. It could be Lithuanian or Romanian. It seemed to him a crazy world that made it practical for people to come all the way to Cornwall to pick daffodils; while the wage wasn't enough to pay the rent and feed your family when you lived here. He supposed it was no different from the countless times that Cornish miners had emigrated because the mines weren't making money. It seemed to him that being global made little sense. Billy Blewett had the right idea, feed yourself and your mates; but not everyone was a good shot like Billy or had green fingers like Billy, and people had lost Billy's knowledge of preparing raw meat for eating.

Daffodil, A Story of Names

As children he and Billy had played in Daffodil, a field where daffodils grew every spring. A tiny field close to the old mill and the old mill stream. The mill hadn't been a mill for years and the water wheel and the mill race were long gone, marked only by the lie of the land and the millstones that leaned against the granite walls of the old mill house. The mill's history was consigned to industrial archaeology, like the mining that had begun even before the birth of the mill. When he and Billy had been boys the mill had been owned by an artist. The footpath down to the valley went down a mile long lane, right past the old mill and across the stream next to a pond, before climbing up into Daffodil. The water travelled down from the moors and gathered pace after the pond as it dived down the valley to the cliff at River Cove.

Daffodil was really just a bit of scrub on the other side of the valley. Cows grazing on the higher moorland fields beneath Rosewall Hill were let down to drink at the pond. Badgers had a huge sett in the scrubby blackthorn rising away towards the moor and the carn and brought their young out to play in Daffodil; until summer visitors from a cottage nearby found out and came to badger watch. From then on the shy creatures stayed away.

Billy Blewett's dad had planted daffodils once as a crop, and from then on they returned in greater numbers each year. The field was too small to plough and the daffodils stayed. Once a flat-back lorry, loaded with crates of lemonade, had somehow come into the lane and kept going down, past the farmhouse, past the mill, so far down that the driver found himself stuck in Daffodil on the far side of the pond. Billy's dad had to pull him out with his tractor.

Today, in the world of contract farming, it seemed that every field was a daffodil field. He pondered the identification of fields. In childhood the fields had either had ancient names or names they'd made up like Daniel's Well, because Daniel had almost fallen down into it; Furzy Down, because it was nothing but gorse and bramble; Swamp field, where they'd played pirates and adventurers in the swampy lake that appeared after heavy rain; Skull Rock where he'd found a fox's skull. These were the names known by anyone of his generation who lived on this stretch of coast. There were other names too: Goat Hill, Long Meadow, Coffin Walk, Sheep Down, Longfield, Hilly Field, Barn Close, Little Down and Witches Rock. The stories behind these fields belonged to earlier generations.

Erosion

The large cultivated fields could hold no more water. For several seasons the natural drainage, the stones of the earth, had been dug out and piled in corners before the crops were sown. The water seeped out from the fields and onto the roads, field water carried débris from the fields and many of the road drains could not cope with the excesses of Nature.

The water leaked into the foundation of Dry Field Hedge. The more saturated the land became, the higher the water rose. It leached in beneath the grounders, found passage through

21

abandoned warrens, formed runnels alongside the stones which had been loosened by roots. Water squeezed wherever it could and in time the stones began to shift, the upper courses slipped and dislodged into the new gaps made in the lower part of the hedge. Between the stones a lump of something other than granite, a buried secret, shifted in the earth.

Everyone looked out at the rain and felt that it was worse than it ever used to be.

Eventually the land dried out and a group of walkers on the Coast Path decided that Zennor was farther than they had thought, so they turned off the Coast Path and headed across the fields towards the road, hoping to find a café. They clambered over Dry Field Hedge into Stony Ground, unaware of the small landslide they caused as stones slipped into a rabbit hole which had been widened by water. The last of the walkers dislodged two stones on the top of the hedge as he hauled himself across it and his arm caught in trailing ivy and blackthorn. He shook it loose and the little cup nest of the Dunnock tore in half and the yellow snail that had been resting beneath an ivy leaf, dropped down a crevice and landed upon decaying sacking.

The One who Stayed

From the seaward side of Dry Field hedge Eddie senses his big brother's presence nearby. He pushes a stone into its place and rests his hand on it as he glances over the hedge and up towards the copse. His eyes look out from under the cap pulled low over his forehead, he recognises the gait of his brother as he steps out of view behind the blackthorn hedge of Fuggy Du. Standback always had to make an entrance. Always made an exit too, he couldn't do anything in a direct way. He couldn't just walk straight across Fuggy Du and down through Longfield. He had to go round by the house. Eddie wasn't surprised, his big brother always had to go his own way. If a gang of boys had gone sledging, his brother'd be the one who made his own run. He was a loner. Awkward bugger more like, always had his own way to do everything. That was his big brother. There was a right way, a wrong way, and Standback's way. Father used to say that about Jack Dash. "Go his own way Jack do," he'd say. "A lone wolf." Well that was fine. There was something of the loner in Standback. Managed to be a loner even when you were with him somehow, just like Jack Dash.

For a moment Eddie regretted his plan.

Cześć

The picker wore a cap to keep her hoody over her head, and the front of the hood stood proud so that she viewed the rows of daffodils as through a funnel that kept the biting south-east wind from her face. She bent, picked the stems, bound them and continued as she chatted with the picker working ahead of her. Standback fell into step, walking along the field edge abreast of the picker. He thought he recognised some of the words and he decided to find out where she came from. The girl became aware of his walking along at her pace and she looked across at him.

He caught her glance and called out to her, "Cześć!"

She looked away and didn't respond.

He tried again, this time he annunciated the foreign word as he had done when Jack had taught him how to say 'Hello' in Polish.

"*Ch..esh..ch!*"

She picked up her pace, moving in rhythm: bending, picking,

banding, stretching, bending. She didn't look up. She had no time for pleasantries.

He turned and left the field. Almost immediately she called out to her friend a few yards ahead of her and their conversation resumed.

Perhaps they were not Polish, perhaps they were Romanian. Suddenly he felt helpless and then he felt guilty. He felt almost as guilty as he had felt at Corpus Christi Fair.

Billy Blewett hadn't suffered with guilt. Billy Blewett had believed that the law of life was to be true to oneself. "I live my life an' I leave other people live theirs," he'd said.

Billy Blewett's Land

Billy Blewett had carved his kingdom in a hollow between the hedges. He'd used his old tractor to clear the tangle of gorse and blackthorn in a lost mediaeval cliff field. There was no romance to it. He roped the spindly trees to the tractor and rooted them out, allowing thorn to grow only on the hedge top. He rotavated the earth into submission for rhubarb, carrots, lettuces, cabbage and his little greenhouse, which he tucked into the corner of the sunny side of his field.

On the shadow side of his kingdom, he had a wire enclosure: a cage with ducks and hens pecking in the mud . . . Grand Saxony ducks with tufted crowns and little Silkies pecking side by side. They were all protected by a low volt electric fence running from a tractor battery beneath a blue tarpaulin. Also, running along the edge of the cage at intervals, were sections of plastic gutter pipe, filled with poison: "For the rats," he'd say. "Kills 'em. Dead."

Billy Blewett's land had strong defences. The blackthorn-covered hedge; a terrier, his constant companion, who would come from nowhere should you veer up the badger track into the hedge. And if you dared to go into the hedge, you faced the unruly barbed wire on top, and the rickety iron ladder descending at a slant on the other side into Billy's slaughter-house. He would always leave the limp bodies of rabbits stretched out at the foot of the ladder.

In the darkest corner of the shadow side of Billy Blewett's land stood two hutches giving off a distinctive smell, and the sound of constant skittering as the ferrets charged the mesh. A golden dog ferret in one; a jill, grey and delicate, and her larger son, grey and white, in the other.

When Billy opened the ferret cage, the ferrets would bound out at a leap. They ran along the top of the hutch, up his arm, round his shoulder, staying close to the source of food. At the bottom of the cage lay the ochre brown and bloody skin of their last meal of rabbit.

Death and Life walked hand in hand in Billy Blewett's land.

Billy had tried to persuade Standback to stay. "If I can do it, you can," he'd said. But Standback was set on leaving. "I can't work with my brother no more," he'd said.

He'd looked around Billy's land and knew it was too closed in for him. He needed air, he needed to get out from a place where he no longer felt at home. Cornwall no longer fitted him. He had to get away.

"You an' me is loners," said Billy, "but we d'have each other's back when we have to."

They'd swapped addresses and phone numbers and he'd gone to Bristol. It was only when he was away that he realised that Billy really was his best friend, and he started to send him postcards from Bristol, then from Southampton, where he worked on the docks, and then from Bristol again. He sent the postcards to Billy at Billy's aunty's house and Billy sent him a

b

card every Christmas; he'd even managed to send a card this last Christmas. It made him chuckle to think of Billy writing his message on the back of his aunty's card. Billy had been recycling all his life.

It was a rough and ready kingdom. It was less than a mile from the road and the picnic lay-by of Rosewall Hill, deep in the tranquil postcard view, Billy Blewett's kingdom was in a thousand photo albums and nobody had ever seen it.

In the summertime Billy often slept there. In the winter he would sleep in his Land-Rover or at his Aunty Rose's home, a little cob cottage on the outskirts of St. Just. Rose had told Standback that Billy had come in one night in February and said he was feeling tired. He went to bed early and didn't wake up. He'd had a heart attack in his sleep. He'd left a message on the bedside table. It said, "Send this to Standback. Tes for the ferrets. This is the address."

He loved his ferrets, he would never use them to catch rats; "They was bitten by a rat, they'd die," he'd said.

The Ferrets

As soon as he'd climbed the ladder down into Billy Blewett's land, the ferrets had started to skitter and chase in their cage. They'd not been fed for almost two days. "A ferret can go twenty-four hours without food providing he d'have water," Billy had once told him. "I knaw some as feed 'em freeze-dried food but that's like 'crack' to ferrets. They get so stuck on it they'll starve their-selves to death. A good ferret an' a shotgun an' you won't never starve in the country."

Standback dropped a dead rabbit into the cage. The ferrets didn't seem to behave any differently after their dry food diet.

Billy had prepared for his death. He'd butchered his birds

and sold them for Christmas. He left his terrier to his aunty, for he knew that although she always grumbled at the dog, she loved it really and it would remind her of her nephew: but he didn't have the heart to kill the ferrets. They were good ferrets. He didn't have the heart to let loose such good ferrets. He'd chuckled as he wrote the note for his friend. "That bastard Standback got to come back home now."

The ferrets ate their fill and Standback opened the cages. They jumped out onto his shoulder, ran up and down his arm. They had no scruples about their new benefactor, one human was as good as another. Only two now, but clearly from the dynasty of golden dog and grey jill.

He'd toyed with the idea of taking them back to Bristol on the train but he'd given them to John Matthews in the pub after the funeral.

"You gotta admire Blewett," said John. "He was a character. Some d'say he was a bit mad like, but I think he was sane as you an' me."

"Saner," said Standback.

Where the Cow Scratched

The stone had been standing upright in the middle of Stony Ground for years. No one knew why it was there. It was granite land, and over the ages granite had been used to build dwellings, hedges for the beasts, hill forts for defence, stone circles, standing stones, burial chambers, fogous, and scratching posts. Billy Blewett's dad had a pretty strong agricultural argument for the origin of the fogou. "Tes a place for the boar in winter," he'd said. "Had to be stone 'cos boars dig see. You back it in an' block up the front. Roll a stone across . . . even a boar can't chew through granite. Keep him there til Spring." It was as good as many stories Standback had heard about the ancient sites. In the 1960s people had gone mad for the stone circles and iron age villages. They'd come down with their cameras to take pictures of the scratching stone. "A sun dial," they said. "A giant phallus," they said. "Rituals," they said. "Pity the stone circle's gone," said those who knew they were experts. "Sad to see the standing stone all alone." "Never was no stone circle." Said Billy Blewett's dad. Maybe there had been and maybe there hadn't; but stones in a field are a pain in the neck if you're ploughing in any century, and stones would be grubbed up and chucked on the hedge. Billy Blewett's dad got so fed up with the hippy philosophers, pagans and would-be historians that he grubbed up the scratching stone. It was an action taken not entirely without anxiety. He wondered briefly whether he might bring down some curse upon the land by moving an ancient religious icon. But he grubbed it out all the same. The following morning, when the cows went out into Stony Ground, Molly (the leader of his herd) wandered straight over to the old stone where it lay across the hedge and rubbed herself happily; Billy Blewett's dad felt it was a good sign. Grandad had been furious because it was a shared hedge, a boundary hedge between Carn and Trevarnon farms.

Over the years the extra weight of the scratching stone, together with the weathering of the rain pouring down the fields from Rosewall Hill and running under the hedge; and the generations of rabbits who burrowed into the hedge, and the roots that pushed through the stones; well, over the years the hedge sank, bulged and re-settled. Grandad got Jack Dash to repair it, one of the last jobs he'd done. When he'd finished the repair, Jack took away the scratching post and made a gate post out of it.

Threads – i

Eddie was growing angry. He was aware of his brother's approach but he couldn't look up. It was like the day after Boxing Day all over again. Anticipation and disappointment all at once. Suddenly he was re-living his eight-year-old self.

He'd often gone out with his father and Standback while they were working, but always on sufferance, sometimes he'd get to fetch and carry but mostly he was sent off to play. However, on Boxing Day his father had said, "Time you started to be a hedger, Edward, see if you've been watching me and Benjamin properly. We'll start on that old hedge on Treveal cliff tomorrow."

He'd felt six feet tall. He couldn't wait to show his father that he had been watching. He'd watched carefully and he knew what to do; but the day had been a complete disaster. He might as well not have been there. His father barely spoke to him and Standback had been dark and surly. That day on Treveal Cliff, which should have been his special day, that day after Boxing Day had been ruined by his big brother.

Eddie had been woken early with the sound of something falling in his parent's bedroom and raised voices; followed later by his father and Standback shouting in the hall, until finally the front door slammed. Things hadn't improved when they had arrived back for supper. Mother had looked tired and pale and she hadn't joined them to eat. He'd followed his mother into the kitchen. He found her sitting at the big scrubbed table and crying as she stared at a pile of tangled cotton reels, pin cushions, scissors, buttons on cards, zips and darning wool.

"It's all such a mess," she said as she dried her eyes. His mother cradled her sewing basket, he could see bits of paper pattern, recipes and old photographs at the bottom of it.

"Was that what I heard this morning?" Eddie asked. "When you and Father were arguing."

His mother looked at him, "Yes," she said. "I knocked the dressing table and my sewing basket fell off and emptied all over the floor, and it woke up your father, you know how lightly he sleep."

"Since the war," said Eddie.

"Yes," his mother put her arm around him, "the war has a lot to answer for," she said.

Eddie sat down beside her, "I'll help you," he said. He picked up a reel of red cotton and began to untangle its thread. He liked the colour red. When he'd separated the red thread from the others he began to wind it back onto the reel. His mother hugged him and smiled and he began to feel whole again as he sat with his mother reeling in the threads.

He didn't notice when his mother got up to go to the range where she hooked up the fire lid and emptied the bits of paper and photos into the flames.

From Opposite Sides of the Hedge

His brother was putting in the second course above the grounders. The repair was looking good but there was something clumsy about the hedger's movements. Eddie turned back to the pile of granite to pick up the next stone. He leaned down to pick it up; he was using his left hand; he handled the stone deftly, holding it close to his trunk, knees bent, he turned back to the gap in the hedge and placed it. He didn't quite set it right first time and turned it slightly. "Not like you Eddie," thought the watcher. As the thought came to him, Standback realised what was wrong. Eddie was working with his left hand, and Eddie wasn't left-handed. His right hand jacket sleeve was tucked into a belt around his coat. From where he stood, at the far end of Longfield, Standback couldn't see his brother's right hand, he seemed hardly to be using it at all.

Beneath his cloth cap Eddie sensed the eyes of his big brother looking down on him but he would not look up. He continued to labour at the stones, as if oblivious to his older brother's presence. He pretended not to see him, even when he could hear his boot steps on the dry earth. It was fifteen years since they had seen each other, suddenly he found himself feeling as raw and hurt as he had when his brother had left for Bristol.

The 15 Year Gap

There was six years between them, but the gap was bigger than the years. The elder brother could remember the war, even though he had been young at the time. He remembered it through the memories of their father and grandfather who still spoke of it, and because of the ration cards that he saw in his mother's handbag. He remembered it because he remembered his father's return in 1948. His father had been missing, believed dead, since late December 1944, just after Christmas leave. No one knew he'd been in a German prisoner of war camp. No one knew because his father had lost his memory. Standback remembered more about Grandad and Jack Dash than Eddie did. Later in life the gap widened when Eddie was married and when, soon after his marriage, Eddie left the farm and moved to St. Just and went to work as a miner. The gap became worse still when their parents died; first their father and not long afterwards, their mother. The United Kingdom entered the EEC, or Common Market as it was to begin with, and the farming landscape changed. Farms that had been handed down through the generations for hundreds of years suddenly became non-viable and the thread of the farming families frayed and finally broke.

"What you doin' up here Eddie?" he asked.

"Waitin' for you," said Eddie.

The eyes of the brothers met across the hedge.

Eddie undid the jacket button of his coat to reveal the sling on his right arm.

"I need a hand," he said.

The Courgette

They worked on the damaged hedge. One either side in the traditional way. Although he couldn't admit it to his little brother, Standback had missed hedging. He had an affinity with stone. Despite Eddie being hampered by his arm, he was far from incapable. Nonetheless, they were like two wild animals forced to share a space. Eddie was talking. Eddie always talked when he was nervous. He couldn't help it.

"It was the judge see, she started it. If she had'n come up with her suggestion, woulden never have happened, but she had to do it. You knaw the sort, got herself made secretary up the allotment, then started checkin' up on all the rules. Said no one shoulden never drive on site, well how else you get a rotavator onto your plot?"

Standback interrupted him, "What you on about, Eddie?"

"Me an' John Matthews had joint first prize, up the produce show. Then this judge, toity maid from over Hayle. She says, 'We'll have a decider. I'll give first prize to the one who gives me the best recipe using courgettes.' You knaw what that John Matthews say? He say 'Courgette do make a bit diff'rant pasty.' An' she give him first prize!"

Standback was still working, "What recipe you give?"

"Didden. Coulden think of one. Hate courgettes anyway. So, when I saw John in the pub after he said he'd done it for a laugh like. 'You're laughing at yourself,' I said. Well, he was taking the piss out his own culture wadden 'ee?"

Standback still didn't look up. "What he say?"

" 'I'm being ironical,' he says. 'How don't we arm wrassle for the prize?' "

Standback looked across to Eddie. "Don't s'pose he was bein' ironical 'bout that."

"No he weren't," said Eddie.

There was a pause.

"How many years John been champion then?" Standback asked.

"Since you left."

Standback grinned.

The Hosken Boys – ii

They shared so many memories and yet they were so different. It bothered both of them. They worked in unison and there was no question about how to set the stones. Everyone said, "If you want a hedge mended or built you get the Hosken boys." It had always been a marvel to the farmers of West Penwith that the two brothers, so different in temperament, should build so well together. It caused many discussions, always terminating in acknowledgement that "S'pose there idden no surprise in that, there are two sides to hedge after all." The Hosken Boys were not of the generation who had gone to the competitions and won certificates for their hedge building. Grandad had been a champion, so had their father, as a young man, before he'd been in the war. Standback stared at the stones.

"Jack was the last person to work on this hedge," he said.

33

Threads – ii: The First Time

It had been snowing overnight. Standback had watched the white flakes against the window until he finally fell asleep. By morning a light covering of snow lay over the yard and across Home Field, Meadow Field and as far as Longfield and Bramble on the cliff.

He'd been longing for the day after Boxing Day. Jack Dash had arranged with Tom Stevens to go out in Tom's boat, and Standback and Tom's son Jim were going too. It would be his first time properly at sea. Uncle Jack had said they might even catch some whiting, but the main aim of the trip was to see the seal pups.

"You have to do exactly what Jim's dad says," he'd said. "There'll be a big sea after the storm on Christmas Day. "We must be on the quay at 5.30 tomorrow morning for the tide."

The night before he'd laid out his warm clothes, wet weather gear, boots, thick socks, and the new Christmas gloves from his Grandad. He'd hardly slept for excitement tinged with fear. He felt his childish fear again as he replayed the events in his mind. He'd hoped he wouldn't be sea-sick. Jim'd said he was bound to get sea-sick because he'd never been proper fishing.

At 4 a.m. he got dressed. He shut his bedroom door quietly so as not to wake anyone and tiptoed down the stairs in his woolly socks. As he opened the back door to go into the yard, his father's voice boomed out, "Where do you think you're going, Benjamin?"

"Goin' fishing with Mr Stevens. We're goin' to look at seal pups. Uncle Jack arranged it."

His father looked angry, "He had no business to. You're comin' hedging with me an' your brother."

"But Da! Tes all arranged."

"Well I'm un-arranging it."

"But you knaw I was going fishing."

"Not any more you're not! Your brother wants to go hedging."

Standback railed at the injustice. "I'm fourteen. I can do what I like!"

The argument escalated too fast; there was no going back for either of them. He had never before blatantly defied his father and it shocked them both. Each knew in his own way that it was a big moment and they had to see it out. They were united in their anger and frustration and could not see that it came out of love.

The father caught hold of his son's arm. "Come with me!" he said.

His son allowed himself to be dragged out through the door and across the icy yard to the barn. He had never seen his father so angry. He was flung to the ground.

"Take off your coat!" For a moment he thought his father was going to beat him and it filled him with fear.

"Why?"

"You think you're so growed up." His father was rolling up his sleeves.

"Da? What are you going to do?"

"It's more what are you going to do!" answered his father. "You reckon you're so growed up. Take off those gloves." In the moment of hesitation he felt his new gloves pulled from his hands and saw them fly over the bales. "Now your coat."

As he pulled off his coat, his father was tugging at bales and pulled them together into a straw table. "You reckon you're so growed up . . . you want to go with Jack Dash so much . . . You wrassle me! You best me, then you can go."

35

The cold flat look in his father's eyes reminded him of when they had first met when his father had come home after the war. The older man leaned against the straw bales, ready and waiting for his opponent. It was unfair, it was unkind, and it was all his little brother's fault. Eddie would have whined, cajoled and nagged their father. Eddie hated it when Father and Standback did things alone. Then another voice came into his head, 'I'm younger than him,' it said, and 'I've beaten most of the boys at school at arm wrestling, including Jim Stevens and he's tough.'

They grasped hands. He was ready. He knew his father was strong and he braced himself. He pushed and pushed, the veins were sticking up in his arms and then the older man's resistance suddenly left as his father's arm dropped a little. He'd done it. He grinned from ear to ear and became victim of the older man's tactical experience as his father took back the advantage, swung with all his might, and flattened Standback's right arm against the straw.

"Your brother's waiting," he said.

The Cornish Hedge

The strength of the hedge starts with the grounders, the foundation stones. The huge boulder-like stones set at the foot of the hedge. From the grounders you build up in rows, or courses, the stones getting progressively smaller until you get to the top of the hedge.

The Cornish Hedge is not like the dry stone wall from the Cotswolds or the North of England. It is not like the stone walls of Ireland, Scotland, or the volcanic boulder hedges of Sicily. Indeed those who construct walls and hedges in these other places are equally proud of their own regional distinctiveness. Even within Cornwall, the hedges of West Penwith are different from the slate hedges to the north of the county with their own alternate 'jack and jenny' herring-bone design of left sloping and right leaning stones. The hedges of West Penwith are stone hedges. They may grow an adornment of bracken, gorse, or blackthorn, and their sloping sides may become covered with plants until they become roadside meadows, but beneath the greenery they are granite. Many unwitting visitors, believing the hedges to be soft grass and fern, move into the greenery to maintain speed in the face of an oncoming vehicle, only to hit the unforgiving granite beneath. Those drivers with knowledge of the Cornish Hedge maintain their distance. They also understand the subtle differences of local stone and style.

With the Cornish Hedge you work to a line, a profile it's called: this gives you the curve, or the batter of the upward rise of the hedge. You have to pack the stones down hard with subsoil, rab is what they call it, never top soil. The width of the base of a good Cornish Hedge is at least equal to its height. The average height is one point five metres from ground level to the top. There's a rough average of a ton of stone to a ton of rab to every cubic metre. However nobody thinks of it in measurements. They think by eye and the knowledge of the forefathers. Cornwall's oldest hedges date back 6000 years. Once you start to read the hedges you can read the history of farming.

The hedger learns his trade by looking and watching. The first lesson is to watch a Cornish Hedger at work. If you look properly at the stones you will learn to pick up the right stone and that's important because the old hedgers say that: "Once you pick up a stone, you've got to use it." They admit that this is an old saying but they tell you that none the less it's the truth. There are so many ways that the amateur hedge builder can create a monstrosity. The average stranger just shoves stones together crudely without looking first. They don't know that every stone has seven faces. They don't know how to listen to the stones, and they'd laugh if you told them that listening to stones was what they should do. Inevitably they end up with hedges which crumble quickly as the elements, the animals, and the natural mathematics of stone take effect.

Those of you who read this and wonder, take a look at some stones. Most stones will have six sides. However, each side has four ways in which it might be placed, four rotations, that makes twenty-four. A choice of twenty-four fits. You see, it's a philosophy. There is a philosophy and a practicality to the trade of hedging. It boils down to the fact that, on average, there's usually no more than seven useful ways to place a stone. It takes time to read stone in this way. The other thing to take into account, when you are repairing, is to learn to read the weather side of a stone, to see the lichen that grows on the weather side. In a good hedge, a hedge that is built right, the weather side is always the smallest face. The big long part of the stone, the part which holds the weight of the stone, that goes down into the inside of the hedge, holding it in place. This is why you have to look at the hedge before you place the stones and you have to look at the stones before you set them in the hedge. It takes time to learn these things. You have to see it all in your mind's eye before you start. This is what the old hedgers believe. If you can do that, if you can see the finished piece, then once built, your hedge will stand for 100 years. This is because every stone has its place, and if you set it wrongly, there will always be a weakness. "Every hole a stone, and every stone a hole": this is another wisdom. This is the art of building the Cornish Hedge.

The Break in the Seam

Eddie liked to give talks up the Old Cornwall Society. He and Standback had argued about it, down in the meadow, the last time they'd worked together.

Standback had been incandescent. He'd tried to explain to Eddie how he felt when he worked with the stones. "You've got to be part of it, Eddie, part of the land. You can't do that from no books and pamphlets and talks. Mebbe he's alright for you Eddie, all they talks up the Old Cornwall an' all . . . you like gabbin'."

Eddie had just stared back at him with the look of an enthusiastic choirboy who simply believed in his truth.

Eddie knew his brother could wind words into strange meanings. He couldn't ever be sure which way Standback would go, truth to tell he didn't always understand his brother. There was a wildness in Standback, something dark at his core. His brother was moody, he might walk off in a strop and leave him to finish the hedge alone, or he might stay on to work into the night.

They'd continued working the stones in silence. They were like two parts of the same machine, and yet each one's approach to their work was alien to the other. Standback had moved a little distant to avoid the impending argument.

"They like my talks up the Old Cornwall," Eddie went on. "I tell all Grandad's old stories. They love 'em. It celebrates the trade, helps to keep it alive."

Standback hadn't replied to his brother, but the following day he'd gone up to Billy Blewett's land to say goodbye to Cornwall.

Eddie had expected his brother to return within a few weeks, as he had done in the past, but this time Standback had stayed away.

What Grandad Said

Grandad used to tell about when he was a boy, how he worked at Carn Farm for Old man Blewett, Walter Blewett, Billy Blewett's grandad.

'Juss fourteen I was when Old Man Blewett asked me up Carn Farm. Said he wanted me build a hedge across Sheep Down. Took me two months. Old man Blewett come up every day to watch. Never said nuthen, juss watched for a bit an' then went off. When I'd finished, on the lass day like, Old Man Blewett come up as usual; only this time he put a line along the hedge. Still didden say nuthen an' I'm pleased as punch like. 'What you want me to do tomorrow, Mr Blewett?' I ask. Blewett looks at me an' smiles, 'Don'ee worry, Boy. I got a job for 'ee tomorrow!' An' he's off down the field. Next day, up I go to Carn Farm bright an' early like an' Blewett meets me in the yard. 'What you want me to do today Mr Blewett?' An' Blewett say, 'You go out there an' start.' . . . 'Start what?' I says. Blewett points up Sheep Down. 'Go see,' he says, an' I'm off up Sheep Down. Old man Blewett, he'd only skat down the hedge I'd built. 'I spent months buildin' that!' I say to him. An' Blewett, he says, 'Have to get'n right.' . . . 'How do I knaw when he's right?' I ask. 'You don't knaw now, you never will,' says Blewett.'

Standback had asked Billy Blewett if he'd heard the story but he hadn't. "Must be apocryphal, right?" he'd said to Billy. Billy just shrugged, "True though," he'd said.

Being Different

Standback had always assumed that he and Eddie shared their memories because they shared their lives; because they were brothers. He was the oldest by six years but that wasn't so much. Once they went to school the gap widened. Eddie had his first year in primary school just as Standback had failed his eleven plus and was going to secondary school in Penzance. He would leave school at fourteen, most farmers' sons left at that age in the 1950s; they had jobs waiting for them on the family farm. They were young men at 14 and 15. Popular culture was just creating a new term, the teenager. Some of Standback's friends from Penzance were Teddy boys. They adopted the quiff, wore drape jackets and crepe soles. They were proud, and members of their own tribe.

It was while he was in his first term at big school that Standback had the first of two important battles about 'tribal difference'.

Difference had started when he went to the village school, boys and girls were in different gangs, they had special play areas. There was a secluded place called 'the girls' side', where girls could do handstands and the boys wouldn't see their knickers, unless they happened to look up from playing marbles beneath the great chestnut tree in the corner of the gravel playground at the right moment. There were also the 'different' children. The Tig boys, gippos from a caravan, swarthy and generally not picked for any communal games sides, unless Mr Pardoe, the teacher, forced the issue. If you'd asked any of the children why this was so, they'd just say, "They're Gippos." There was no real malice. The Tig boys knew they were different, they separated themselves from everyone anyway. There was Mad Herbert who used to direct traffic that had no need of being directed. He wore an old army great-coat and the kids taunted him by jumping out screeching from behind trees to set him off. Mad Herbert's eyes looked wild and he'd do a mad dance, running every which way. Much later in life Standback had realised that Herbert suffered shell shock in the First World War. Then there was Cakeplate, that's what they used to call Uncle Jack, because of the cut-out doilies he used to make. Sometimes they called him Doily Jack. They said he was a German Prisoner of War. He was a Polish European Volunteer Worker but the classroom heard his foreign voice and said he was a German spy.

Standback had been a bit late picking up his little brother after school. He'd found Eddie surrounded by a whole group of children and Eddie was telling about the rats.

"He used to eat rats," he was saying. "That German POW. I'd rather die than eat rats, woulden you?" His audience was making the appropriate gagging grimaces and noises. "I seen him cook one," said Eddie.

Standback grasped his little brother's collar. "Liar!' he said.

"Am not, I did see him cook one."

Standback yanked the collar until Eddie was on tiptoe. "See him kill it?" Eddie shook his head. "See him skin it?" Eddie shook his head. His face had turned crimson. Standback held fast to Eddie's collar as he said, "Wadden no rat then was a?"

"Yes it was! He was tellin' all about the camp in the snow an' how they caught'n an' ate 'em."

The crowd of boys stood in amazement, watching the two brothers. Standback swung round at them. "It'd be rabbit. He'd be tellin' about the rats but he be cookin' rabbit. Jack said he woulden never eat no rat again, not so long as he lived. He coulden do it. Not 'cos a rat idden meat but 'cos it made him feel degraded. Thass what Uncle Jack said! An' he idden no German neither; fact he flew bombers on our side, an' he's here as a volunteer worker! He work on our farm."

There was a hush from the crowd of boys who saw their teacher approaching behind Standback.

"What's going on here? Release that boy. Stand back there!"

42

Mr Pardoe, the Headmaster, bore down on the Hosken brothers.

"You know the rules about fighting! However, I can't punish you as it's after school time and one of you no longer attends. But . . ." He held the group of boys in his most icy glare. "Any more such behaviour and I shall speak to your parents. All of your parents." He eyed the crowd of boys sternly. They were silent as Mr Pardoe held them in his gaze. Then the headmaster wheeled around and put his hand on Standback's shoulder.

"Well said, Benjamin. A fine example of how not to stand back in the face of untruth. Let this be a lesson, boys. Right. Home, all of you!"

The name Standback had stuck to him and he had become another outsider because he was a friend of Cakeplate, the German spy.

The View from Two Sides

He'd forgotten how Eddie would never let things go. How his brother would keep on and on at him, prise out his inner feelings before even he himself had worked them out. The end result was always the same, he would reply through accusation. Eddie cajoled; their father had rebuilt this ancient hedge with Grandad. It was right that they, the sons and grandsons, should do the repairs today.

"We can do it right, Standback, you an' me together."

And they could, he was right, everything Eddie said was right. It was what he didn't say, the thing he wouldn't acknowledge, that was what stood in the abyss between them.

"This used to be ours, Eddie!" There, he had said it.

Eddie nodded. So Standback still nursed the old hurt. He

43

sighed and returned the old argument, "Farm coulden support one man, let alone two."

"One man live there now!" He'd walked into it; they would replay their differences.

"He's paid to manage it."

"We could've managed it, Eddie."

"How could we?"

"Estate agent's son, what he knaw about farming?"

"He idden farming. It's land management. Barron have to look after all the footpaths, stiles, signs, the whole coastline."

"Used to be three farms up 'ere, Eddie. Mr and Mrs Blewett up the Carn, Harry Trengrouse at Chy Tolver, an' we at Trevarnon. He's livin' in my house!"

The wound between them yawned and gaped. They'd got to it quickly. He'd wondered whether this time might be different. Fifteen years ago they'd had the same argument.

Everything looked the same but everything was different. The world had changed. Soon, even Billy Blewett's land would be brambled over and become just another thicket, as it had been for centuries in the past before Billy Blewett reigned.

'Dish o'Tay?'

They worked on in silence for almost an hour. This was a conversation with no disagreement. They knew how the hedge should be. They knew the order of the stones. They were speaking the same language and were in accord. They worked this way until noon. A time they knew by the height of the sun, the light in the sky, the song of the birds, and the feeling in their bones. They knew the time in the same way that the birds and insects and beasts did. They lived it.

Standback was aching. Perhaps he'd gone soft up Bristol. His most recent work had been a driving job, nine months sitting in a van cab up and down the M5. Hands gone soft too. The sun was higher in the sky. They had worked solidly. He had to admit that Eddie was keeping up with him despite his arm. He stood up, straightened his back, and stretching backwards he looked up over towards Longfield. The pickers had moved across the road to another field. Some of them were leaning against one of the convoy of white vans, fagging up and taking a quick tea break.

Eddie pulled a flask from his canvas rucksack and poured out a cup of tea.

"Dish o' tay?" Eddie handed his brother a mug of red tea. "Reckoned you woulden've brought any with you."

Standback took the mug.

"Cheers."

"Got a pasty, you want one."

"Mebbe later," said Standback. It irked Standback that Eddie had been so sure of his brother's help that he'd come prepared; but it also felt so natural to be amongst the stones on Trevarnon Farm. He squatted down on the grass, his back against the piece of hedge he had been working on. He continued to watch the pickers.

Eddie followed his brother's gaze. "Fieldwork go furriners these days. Europeans."

Standback nodded.

Eddie went on, "Been a lot of changes since you went away, Standback. 'Course, biggest change was the seventies and eighties," he paused. "Father woulden recognise Cornwall now, so much change. The bypass over Longrock . . . Remember back along, Finns Shoes? Gone. Hayle 'lectric Works . . . Gone. All the shops in Penzance had local names above the doors. Tes all chain stores, charity shops an' galleries these days. An' remember all they little corner shops we used to have? I

45

sometimes wonder what Father'd think. Thass why I do my talks. I can remember a place that's gone. Things can change but you can't take away a man's whole history. Not so long as we tell the next generation."

Standback drank his tea as he watched the pickers moving back and forth. The wind was still brisk but the sunshine, however weak, raised the spirits and they'd get a bit of shelter when they moved across to Sanctuary.

"I bring children out here sometimes, I done talks in schools too." Eddie was on a roll now. "One thing everyone like is stories about what you find in a hedge. I show 'em flints an' stuff, an' old poison bottles. Remember Grandad telling about the baby he found buried in a hedge one time? Well they like that one. Tes all history."

The pickers were getting ready to move across into Sanctuary.

Was that what he'd become, history?

What Grandad Said

Grandad used to say: *"Nuthen worse'n a hedge've got growth on it. Attracts the rats and rabbits. Rabbits is wurst. You block up a hole, they'll only dig another. Finest thing for a hedge is cut it back tight every year and leave no growth on it at all. That'll get rid of rabbits more'n anythin'. Cut it so tight as possible. Don't leave any cover at all for a rabbit. A rabbit like to look out a hole see if anythin's about. He want to be able to look out an' say 'everything's alright, I can go out now.' If your hedges are bare that'll send 'em goin' somewhere else. You don't b'lieve me; juss take a look at Blewett's hedges. He don't trim no hedges at all. There's growth all over 'em an' he's pestered me with rabbits for years, 'cos all the rabbits d'come over our place don'um? No. Nuthen worse for havin' rabbits than a hedge with growth in it."*

The Rabbit

The Rabbit sat in the pink of an early spring sunset. He looked like a brown stone in the longer grasses close to the base of the hedge. He was perfectly still, every inch of him was alert to the sound of death. It might drop silent and swift from the sky, with the early Barn Owl, or it might come from the snap of the jaws of the Fox as he made his rounds, or from the lead of shot bursting in hot pain through his skin from an unseen enemy behind the blinding white light of lamps. Behind him, in his burrow deep in the hedge, his doe and six kits were warm and safe. The kits would be safe for another ten sunsets and then they would start to forage themselves. They would be joyous up in the air with the new smells, the grass, the scents of other creatures, the wind on their fur and young sweet grass to nibble and chew. Some of them would be taken for prey, for the new young Barn Owls, Kestrels, Buzzards and Foxes would also be out for the first time. It was the way of things in his rabbit world. He was the buck. His whiskers flicked as his nostrils flared and tensed. He stood upright, stock still. His grey-brown fur was well camouflaged against the stones and the winter-brown bracken. His scent whisked away behind him, away from the sound and his sensitive ears were still as he absorbed the sound. Dog, Dog was very close, he heard the panting, the scent was strong in the breeze. Dog was coming. He froze. He heard the whistle, the call of the men with guns. He turned about and bounded down, deep, deep into his burrow, as the dog started to paw at the hole in the hedge.

Treveal Cliff

Eddie was struggling with the sling. Standback watched his brother hoist up a big stone in his left hand, holding it against his chest as he leaned into the hedge to place it. The stone began to slip and instinctively he went to catch it with his injured arm, winced, and the stone almost fell. Standback took it from him and laid it in its place.

"Thanks," said Eddie. He paused. "Remember first time Father took us hedging?"

Standback thought about it but he couldn't answer.

"Treveal Cliff," said Eddie.

"That wasen first time!"

Eddie ignored him, "I thought it'd be just me an' him."

Standback realised that he and Eddie had never really spoken of that day. "You kept on an' on at him," he said, "made him take the both of us. I only had a pair of old socks for gloves. I'd had a lovely new pair of gloves off Grandad for Christmas but Father chucked them over behind the bales."

Eddie carried on, "Father says, what you notice boys?"

" 'My bleddy hands're comin' off's' what I wanted to say," said Standback. "Fourteen year old I was. I stood up to him though. 'You got to look first,' I say, 'an' then go to a heap of stone, pick one up an' he'll fit exactly, stone on stone,' an' he's there lookin' at me, his eyes bright with knowin', an' he says, 'When you can do that, boy, you can build a hedge. Buildin' hedge idden nuthen once you can do that.' "

Eddie was staring at him.

"You weren't though."

"Weren't what?"

"Lookin'."

Standback met his brother's eyes, "What you mean, not lookin'?"

"You weren't lookin' at the stones. You was watchin' Tom Stevens' boat!"

Tom Stevens' boat. Tom had come right in close to the rocks off Seal Island, close enough for Uncle Jack to see the seal pups.

"I was the one lookin'," said Eddie.

Standback became aware of his brother, "What make you remember that?"

Eddie continued, "Father said you was a natural. Didden say nuthen to me."

"Fought me every inch of the way. Made me wrassle him that morning."

"I didden knaw that."

"Why would you? You was only eight. More he tried to rein me in, more I wanted to break out."

Their father had handed him a cup of tea, told him to 'catch hold an wrap his hands around the tin mug' so that his frozen fingers had screamed with the pain of thawing on the hot tin. His father had done it on purpose.

Eddie was still talking, "He allus took an interest in you," he said. "Father allus wanted you close. But you was allus up Jack Dash's hut."

"He put up with Jack 'cos Jack was Grandad's right hand man end of the war. But Tom Stevens' boy Jim'd just been done for breaking into Harvey's tobacconist. That's what Dad minded," said Standback.

The Best of it

It seemed to Standback that his little brother had always had the best of it. He'd been born after the dark days of their father's

49

return from the German prison camp and the hospital. He'd benefitted from his father's experience of his eldest son's growth into manhood. To Standback it seemed that Eddie had never had arguments with his father in the way that he had done. Eddie seemed charmed. Besides Eddie hadn't stayed on the farm. In the 1970s Geevor Tin Mine had been prosperous and Eddie had turned to mining. He'd married, and his wife had benefitted from his miner's wage packet, so the only time he might have considered farming she was dead against it; by then Eddie had two kids as well. Eddie was the steady one, he passed his eleven plus, just; he joined clubs, orienteering; nowadays the Old Cornwall Society and the Local History Society. He'd even travelled farther than Standback ever had. Eddie had been on a package holiday to Spain, to Loretta del Mar. The farthest Standback had travelled was to Southampton, where he'd worked on the docks. He'd stayed in boarding houses with sailors, drunk with them and occasionally fought with them. He'd listened to sailors from Tangier, Shanghai, San Francisco, and in that way he knew the world. Eddie could talk of the unfinished hotels, the food, the bulls and flamenco, but he looked into himself and decided that St. Just was the best place to be. Standback was restless, happy anywhere and nowhere in particular. He knew the world as he knew the men and women who lived in it. Somehow, although he knew he belonged in the granite land of his birth, he also belonged to a body of people who stood apart and alone and watched. Language was no barrier to Standback unless it was the language of paper forms and government directives.

Horsepower – i

Engines were measured by horsepower for many years; some still talk of horsepower; even though it's a long time since horses pulled more than a ceremonial coach. The great Shires, on occasion, come out for fêtes, sometimes a ploughing match, but they are fewer and fewer in number each year.

In the 1920s the average power of tractors was 25 horsepower. The first 'Big' tractor in Britain came from Fowlers in Leeds and was developed from Britain's First World War tanks. Tractors became bigger and more powerful in the 1970s, as much as 420 horsepower. These days tractors have front and rear steering, hydraulics, suspension. The dealers talk of EPM (engine power management), SCR (selective catalytic reduction), DOC (diesel oxidisation catalyst), and EGR (exhaust gas re-circulation). They also cost hundreds of thousands of pounds.

Inside the cab, these tractors look like aircraft cockpits. Not only have they got cabs, they are also technologically at the top of their game. These mammoth beasts can travel fast. They are too big for the lanes. Too big for the old fields and gateways. Their big wheels grind at the foot of the Cornish hedges and the grounder stones are loosened.

Suddenly the tractor has become a monster engine with space-age facilities. Grandfather's TE20, which had hauled, ploughed and done everything on their farm for years, 'The Little Grey Fergie', invented by Harry Ferguson, with a Standard engine, sprung seat, in the open air to all weathers, and no onboard radio or music, only the sound of the birds and bees and general occasional traffic; *The Little Grey Fergie* with its petrol engine, 4 cylinders and a capacity of 2088cc.; the tractor which had revolutionised post-war farming, was now a museum piece, lined up at rallies and agricultural shows, alongside the milk-churns, chain harrows and hand-tools that were still occasionally found at the back of old barns.

The Mad Mechanic

Harry Ferguson didn't invent tractors but he invented the world's most famous tractor. He didn't invent flying; but he was the first Briton to build and fly his own plane. He was also one of the three-man team who created the Formula One winning 4 wheel drive car.

Harry, one of 11 children, was brought up on the family farm in Ireland. At the age of 15 he was expected to pull his weight on the farm but Harry described farming as 'murderous work'. Harry preferred tinkering with engines. He went to work in his big brother's garage in Belfast, convincing his brother that entering motor-cycle races would be good publicity for the garage which soon had a reputation for fine-tuning engines. Not one to stand still Harry became interested in flying, convincing brother Joe that it would also help the garage business if they could build and fly planes. In 1909 he took his monoplane into the air, some nine to twelve feet off the ground, and flew 130 yards into gusty winds.

In 1928 he put in a patent for Three Point Linkage. This hydraulic system enabled tractors to hold implements such as the plough, rather than haul them. On the 6th July 1946 the first of the TE20s, with the Standard Vanguard engine, came off the line of the factory in Coventry which had previously been an American shadow factory producing aero engines for the British government during the war. When the factory closed at the end of the war Harry took the opportunity to strike a deal. TE stood for Tractor England, previously the tractor engines had been imported American ones (1966cc Continental Z-120). By 1949 Ferguson tractors held around 78% of the tractor market. By 1956, when the last TE20 rolled off the line, the total number of TE20s produced (including variants) was 517,651.

The boy who considered farming to be 'murderous work' had revolutionised agriculture.

Harry, together with Claude Hill and Tony Rolt, began work on a four wheel drive car engine, the P99. In 1961 the P99 won the Grand Prix at Oulton Park. It was driven by Stirling Moss. Sadly Harry died in 1960 and didn't see the success of the P99.

Horsepower – ii

Everything about modern farming is bigger than it used to be. Farming is an Industry. A big Industry. In order to meet the demands of the late 20th and the 21st century, the farms are no longer mixed. The days of chickens in the yard, dairy cattle in the meadow, sheep on the hills, and corn, silage, root crops; these are pictures for jigsaw puzzles. The days of milk-churns left on the stand at the end of the lane to be taken to the dairies; these days which Standback could still remember. These days had gone.

The great prairie wheat-fields of Canada and Australia and the United States, with their huge combine harvesters and their crop duster planes, meant that wheat could be grown in such bulk, and sold so competitively, that it was not worth the small farmer's time to grow wheat. In the 1950s and even in the early 1960s you might still have seen hay in stooks in the Cornish fields, and haystacks covered in tarpaulins. Indeed, Mr Uren, who used to keep a chicken farm, one of the first specialist chicken units in the county, still carried buckets of feed in a yoke all the way from his cottage along the road and up the lane to his chicken farm. In the 1950s and 1960s change was still a gradual process. In the childhood of the Hosken boys, there had still been cottages out in the country without mains water and electricity. True, some remained reliant on oil lamps and accumulators longer than most because they were more isolated from the 'grid' but others just enjoyed their warm lamps and sparkling water.

Standback barely recognised the place he had left, change had accelerated.

Lizards & Dinosaurs

They'd been talking about Lizards. Standback had started it. He couldn't help himself. They'd been working together fine, working in silence with just the bird-song, the sound of stones, and the distant sea crashing in the cove, but Eddie just couldn't keep quiet. He had to point out how well they got on when they put their minds to it.

"Like they say, you want a hedge mended or built . . . get the Hosken boys! Instinctive, how we work together. We got a rhythm here," said Eddie.

Standback couldn't help himself. Even as he said it he knew he should have kept quiet, he should have let Eddie stay happy in his brotherliness. But he couldn't do it. He couldn't leave it alone.

"On your own you can move easy, hear the insects an' see wass on round you. Might be a lizard basking. Used to see lizards all the time, loads of 'em. Don't see so many nowadays. You got to love the country you're working with, Eddie. You got to be part of it. You need to listen to it, taste it, not talk about it!"

He couldn't help it. He knew a different way. He couldn't see things in the same way as his brother.

"Seemin' to me it's allus you doin' all the talking," said Eddie.

"I idden talking!" he heard himself shout back, "I'm sayin'."

And he knew it was a distinction that Eddie couldn't see. If only his brother would let it rest. If only Eddie would stop making the difference between them show. If only he'd got on the train for Plymouth instead of coming to work with Eddie. It would have been better if he'd left. Of course it would have been even better if he hadn't reacted, if he could just let it go, but he couldn't.

"When I talk up the Old Cornwall, well, they like to remember. So I tell 'em. It's like Grandad used to say, after the war sons all got on tractors an' no one had no time to hedge no more. It died with the old men."

"Well thass history, Eddie, everythin' change, like it or no."

Eddie ignored him. "It's the flail."

"What is?"

"Why you don't see lizards. Habitat's gone."

"Still water go stagnant," Standback replied.

"You juss said you miss the lizards!"

"I don't miss dinosaurs. If we didden have change we'd be livin' with the dinosaurs. Christ, Eddie! When it come to hedging, it's like Father'd say: 'there's a right way and a wrong way, and everyone have his own way.' You can't put that in no talk. You got to live it!"

"Think I don't knaw that!" Eddie was angry now. "You juss want to have the last word. Don't forget, I knaw you, Standback. You're so sure aren't you? You really think you're right."

"Course I bleddy am. Aren't you?"

"You're not going to make me feel guilty!" said Eddie.

There was a long pause as yet another wound opened. Now

55

they were getting to it. He didn't see why his brother shouldn't feel guilty. Hadn't Eddie always landed on his feet? He hadn't cared about anything as much as Standback had. He didn't feel the land in the same way. He talked the talk at those Old Cornwall nights, but he'd never lived that way. Never.

It was still the same argument, they just got to it by different routes and they played it out over and over again. Each lost in his own guilt, each unknowingly wanting the reassurance of their parents that the loss of the farm hadn't been their fault. After fifteen years they had finally picked up exactly where they had left off.

Mothers and Sons

Standback had been waiting for Eddie for three hours. His mother's mantelpiece clock ticked each second of each minute in the eerie stillness of the farmhouse kitchen. The house felt hushed and silent, apart from the *tick tick tick* of the clock. Eddie would be here soon. It was his turn. The ticking burrowed into his skull and he could hear it as if from inside his head. *Tick tick tick* . . . once he had tuned into the ticking he could not escape it. His body ached for sleep but he must wait for Eddie. He'd been up all night, he was dizzy with tiredness. He opened the kitchen door to the yard and gulped in the cold living air. He had hardly slept for the week, and when he had slept it was only to live through the dream of the hours of wakening. He wandered out of the kitchen into the lounge. Mother always called it the parlour, because that's what it had been when she and his father had been courting. It was cool and dark and he knew that there was a bottle of whisky in the corner cupboard. He didn't even get a glass, just pulled off the top and took a long draught. Eddie hadn't done the nights, he'd gone home; he'd been able to step back into the living world. For Standback the last few months had been all one long dark night. He'd almost finished the bottle when the kitchen door slammed and Eddie came in.

"Yew!" Eddie called into the house as he always did. He breezed in with the living world at his heels. There followed the rattle of plastic bags, the fridge door was opened and closed and the pedal bin lid snapped shut as the plastic bag was thrown in. He could see the familiar actions. Eddie was whistling softly.

Standback stood up, reeled slightly and knocked over the low coffee table. He reached the door into the kitchen and leaned against the frame. Eddie stopped whistling and turned towards his brother.

"You said you'd come back!" said Standback.

"I didden knaw Christine'd have to work late. Then Jen missed the bus home and Tamsyn had gym practice. Time idden your own with teenagers."

Eddie was filling the kettle under the tap in the kitchen sink. Eddie made life sound so normal. It seemed to Standback that his brother's life was like something from a film. It was tidy, everything in its place, entirely different from his own personal chaos.

"You said you'd come back. I had to do everything, everything . . ."

"I rang ten o'clock an' there wasn't no reply. I guessed you'd hit the bottle."

His little brother looked so smug with his organised family and his neat home in St. Just.

"How's she doing, anyway?" Eddie asked.

Standback stared at his brother. "Gone," he heard himself say.

"What? . . . Dead?"

"No, gone Co-op for bread. Course she's bleddy dead."

"I didden knaw."

57

"Course you knew. We talked about it last night, how close it was."

"But we didden knaw. I mean we didden knaw when."

Standback scraped a chair out from the kitchen table and sat down heavily. Eddie went upstairs. The kettle started whistling, Standback watched it steam and then got up and finished making the tea slowly; warming the pot, pouring a fistful of loose leaves straight into the pot, then the hot water, and finally stirring it with a fork that was lying nearby. He carried the teapot to the table and set it on its stand, then he returned to the sink and pulled a couple of mugs from the soaking dishes, rinsed them, shook off the water, and set them with the teapot on the scrubbed table. He waited for his brother to come back downstairs. He would tell him about the box. He'd searched everywhere he could think of and found nothing.

The Box

His mother had asked for a cup of tea. She kept asking for a cup of tea. He would make one and bring it upstairs to her bedroom and she would thank him. "A nice cup of tea," she'd say, and she'd take the cup and have a sip. Sometimes they would talk for a minute or two. Most times she would just stare in front of her and, after a while, she'd hand him the cup and saucer and he would put it on the bedside table with the cup almost full. He'd straighten the pillow while she was sitting up and she'd lie back but she wouldn't sleep. Her eyes would be wide open. Sometimes he would doze off for a second then jerk awake, as if on a long train journey, and when he awoke he would forget for a moment where he was and then he'd see her eyes. She would be lying there with her eyes open. One sip of tea in the very early hours, and at last she slept, it was as though

58

she had reversed the natural sleep-waking hours. These days she was awake all night and would sleep in the day. The woman who had a ticking clock in every room had fallen into her own version of time. He would stare at her. It seemed to him that his mother wasn't there any more, or if she was she was deep deep deep behind her eyes. Perhaps she was in her soul he thought.

He sipped his own tea, it was good and strong, red, just as he liked it. Eddie had made tea just before he'd left the evening before. He hadn't stopped to share a cup, he'd been in a hurry to get home. 'We don't share a cup of tea no longer,' he thought to himself. 'She don't, an' Eddie don't. Cups of tea get made and I allus drink alone.' He stared through the bedroom window and over to the hill with the thicket of trees and the old tin hut. The deep red dawn was turning orange as the sun rose. At last the long night was over. Maybe he too could sleep now.

He took the cups downstairs, returned with a glass of water and leaned over the bed to check on his patient. He felt a vice-like hold on his arm as his mother's eyes opened wide "Benjamin! You don't know! . . . You know, in the war, things were different, not like now. Your father sent postcards from Africa an' India, Scotland too. He hardly ever come home an' it was juss me. Granma and Grandad, they didden know, an' you . . . you were juss little . . . you didden know . . ." She was very breathless, he tried to calm her.

"Shssh," he said. "It's alright, the war's over now."

"No! No!" she said. "You don't know. No one knew. No one ever knew!" She still held his arm in her iron grip. "You don't know what war's like. It changes people."

"I remember when Father come home," he said. "He wasn't the same, didn't look like he did in his photograph."

"No! You don't know! You don't know . . !" she shouted.

59

"You got to sleep, Mum."

"I got to tell you," she said. "The box . . . your father . . . It's in the box. Find the box."

He'd tried looking around the bedroom, but she was getting more and more distraught. Her voice became indistinct as her mouth was dry. He tried to wipe her lips with one of the lemon-flavoured mouth sticks the nurse had left, but she pulled her head away. He marvelled at the strength. He'd seen it before in dying animals, but never in humans. The first time had been as a boy when he'd watched the barn cat play with a mouse; the mouse was so injured that its intestines dragged along outside its body as it ran but still it ran, prolonging its own agony, while the great cat eyes watched. It had horrified him when he saw a rabbit try to jump into the hedge after its back had been broken by a car. Uncle Jack had told him that it was life: "The spirit to live is strong," he'd said. "We cling to life even as it slips from our grasp."

He tried again to moisten his mother's lips and she swung her head again to avoid him and his elbow caught the glass of water on the bedside table and it spilled all over her pillow. The woman who couldn't lift a finger to help herself, who couldn't lift her skirt to go to the toilet, had such force.

"I don't know what you're trying to say!" he shouted. "I don't know what you want! I've never known!" It was out before he could stop it. It was as if the strength of her opened his deep self.

"Your father loved you," she said.

And his deep self answered, "He didn' do nuthen but hold me back! Hung on too long. Allus pushin' me away when I tried to help."

She clung onto him with both her hands, "It was the war!" she said. "You'll understand . . . in the box . . ." and she fell back onto the bed for the last time.

He felt her pulse, closed her eyes and went downstairs. The tap was dripping, *drip, drip, drip* into the plastic washing-up bowl full of tea cups. He turned off the tap. He sat at the kitchen table. The clock on the mantelpiece ticked each second as his mind ran over the last minutes of his mother's life. He had to have some air. He got up to open the kitchen door.

The Cup of Tea

They sat in silence as Standback poured the tea.

"The pillow's wet," said Eddie.

Standback told his brother about the box and their mother's final strength. "You should've come, Eddie, you should've come back."

"I was working. I've got a family, it's hard. . ."

"With a job and a family and a home!" It was the same old argument, as it so often was between them.

"You can't blame me for that."

"There's enough room here at Trevarnon for both of us."

"I got a home in St. Just."

"You mean Christine won't never move."

"Don't bring Christine into it. Anyway, so what if she won't! We've invested a lot in our house; modern kitchen, bathroom, central heating. This old house'd take thousands to renovate. Throw money at it and you woulden never see no diff'rance."

"Perhaps that's what she was on about."

"What?"

"The pillow was wet 'cos she went mad tryin' to tell us something . . ." and he told his brother about the box. "S'posin' there was money in that box, Eddie. S'posin' the old man had money hidden away all this time."

Eddie stared at his brother; "You said yourself she could've been talking about anything. She was rambling you said."

61

They searched the house but didn't find a box of money, or a box that held anything that might have explained their mother's hysteria.

Penmount

Eddie had felt guilty about the hours Standback had spent with their mother. He hadn't been able to cope with death ever since Grandad had told him to watch the sick lamb. "Maybe you can help me feed him later," Grandad had said, but the lamb wouldn't move later, even though Eddie had watched it all the time.

"I'm sorry I coulden do more with Mother," said Eddie. He couldn't express what he really wanted to say.

While his brother was stumbling over words in his mind, Standback spoke coldly, "You don't know what it was like Eddie."

"Don't I? You don't know that!"

"You weren't there!" Standback said.

"Oh yes, you had to do everything! You couldn't take your eyes off her for a second. Standback, you were pissed most of the time back then."

"Never had enough to shut it all out."

Eddie hated it when Standback became morose and sorry for himself. He hit back, "You was so pissed you left her up Penmount alone."

"Wasn't no one there."

"You left our Mother all alone at the crematorium."

"There wasn't no one in that coffin, Eddie . . . juss a . . . a . . ."

"The body of our mother."

"So I went down the road for a drink! So what!"

"You don't get it, Standback, do you? You never did. It's not all about you!"

62

"What d'you mean?"

His brother looked hurt. "Don't do that Standback!"

"What?"

"Pretend you don't understand."

"I don't understand."

And suddenly Eddie understood what he'd always known about his brother but he had never before been able to put it into words. "When you feel guilty, or you can't cope any more, you just run away. You ran away up Penmount. And you ran away up Bristol," he said.

Standback stared at the stone in his hand as if he was trying to see into it. "I'm knackered, Eddie. Been a long couple of days, buryin' Billy Blewett . . ."

Eddie raised his eyes to the heavens.

Standback placed the stone and continued working as he spoke.

"I knaw you didden think much of Billy; but he was a mate. Left me his ferrets. I had to go his place an' fetch 'n. You knaw, Eddie, it was juss as I remembered it, hadden changed a bit. I been up Penzance high street, hardly recognised it. I been down Trevarnon this morning. The house is there but he idden there, not really is'a?"

"Thass what I'm sayin'! . . . Thass why I like to do my talks . . ."

Standback ignored his brother's comment and continued, "Billy Blewett's land, it look exactly the same. Felt the same, even smelled the same."

They worked on in awkward silence. Then Eddie said, "Every hedge have an eye, an' every ditch have an ear . . ."

"Grandad used to say that," said Standback.

63

What Grandad said about Shiners

Grandad had won prizes for his hedging. There had been red and yellow certificates in one of the corner cupboards in the kitchen. Some had faded to illegibility and others had been eaten by silver-fishes. No one noticed because when they looked through the glass they saw what they always saw: Grandad's certificates and Mother's souvenirs from day trips. There was a little brass bell with a brass pixie handle from a day out up Bude; a silver teaspoon from Newquay with a tiny pixie engraved inside the basin of the spoon; and a half tea-cup, just one side of a cup with a flat back and a handle; on the round side it had said 'Half a cup of tea from Land's End'. Mother had enjoyed presenting it to anyone who, when asked if they'd like a cup of tea, responded, 'Well, just half a cup.'

Agricultural Day 1937:
Ploughing, Hedging, Thatching and Points Judging.

Grandad had a yellow certificate for that. He had also won a Special Prize in the West of England Championship in 1947. Grandad had been hedging for longer than anyone and was a judge by then. It was his last competition, he was retiring.

He had the eye did Grandad, he didn't need a line to see if the batter was right, but he did use one for competitions. "Tisn't juss my eye lookin'," he'd say. "Others mightn't see it straight without I put a line along."

Old man Blewett never forgave him for disqualifying him on a shiner.

"Juss a big stone," he'd cried indignantly.

"You can't kid me, Walter Blewett," said Grandad. "That stone's all face an' no back. You knaw a stone that size got to go in at least a foot."

64

"It do," says Blewett.

"Want me dig'n out and prove it?" Grandad asked him. Blewett shut up then. He could still move stone easier than most men, and he would've too, but Grandad was in his prime. Blewett never forgave him though.

Doily Jack

Cakeplate was the other name he'd been given. No one ever called him Jan, which was his real name. They'd called him Uncle Jack at home. Grandad had been the first to call him Jack. His real name from Poland was Jan Daszyński. Grandad decided it was easier to call him Jack Dash. There'd been a Polish girl at school, she used to be called Jenny. She had thick straw-coloured hair which she wore in a single long plait down her back. One day Billy Jenks saw a name tag in the back of her mackintosh. It looked like 'Slobjack'. From then on everyone called her Slobberjack. He talked to Eddie about it. "Remember the Polish girl in my class at school?"

"Slobberjack?" said Eddie.

"Wadden very kind."

"Nicknames never are," Eddie shrugged. "What about Thickneck, or Fatty Stephens, they idden nice. We only called her Slobberjack 'cos of the name in her mac." He paused then laughed, "Remember Smelly Susan? Nicknames, juss nicknames is what they are."

"You never had one, did you?" said Standback.

"Wadden colourful enough I s'pose. What make you talk about all that?"

"Must've been difficult for they Polish kids. They didden ask to come here, some got born here. P'raps your whole family's dead. You woulden know your Granma's house."

Eddie shrugged; "Never thought about it really."

"They came to school. Got laughed at an' called thick 'cos they didn't understand stuff. S'pose you went home an' closed the door an' you were in another country? Think about it, Eddie, behind the door. Different language, different songs. I mean all our lives we lived 'ere," Eddie went to speak but Standback carried on, "I knaw I went away but it's still true, we knaw the hills, the coves. We knaw where to swim, we knaw who own the next farm . . . well we used to . . . we knaw things we don't even knaw we knaw." He was losing himself in his thought and then he stared at the ground and smiled; "Like the foxglove, like the foxglove be the first flower come up on this hedge when he's built!"

"Juss nicknames. No diff'rant from calling Whiteo Fatty or Peter Uren Snotnose. We was kids, didden mean nuthen. Mind that Slobberjack was a smart-arse, ended up standin' for the council. Learned to speak Cornish an' all but she wadden born here so what she knaw?"

"She's lived here long as you have!"

"Idden the same as bein' born 'ere though is'a?"

"Thass what I'm saying. We knaw things we don't even knaw we knaw."

"Yes."

"An she must've known things we don't knaw, like Uncle Jack. Jack was seventeen when the Germans marched into Warsaw, still a kid when he saw his old man shot down."

"You think too much Standback. Allus make a thing complicated."

Synku Mój

Perhaps Eddie was right. Perhaps he had spent his life running away. Hadn't that been what he was doing at Corpus Christi? He'd always justified it because Jack had told him to stay out of it, not to get involved. But had he used it as an excuse? When he'd first left Cornwall, Billy Blewett had said he was running away. Didn't feel like it at the time but he had turned his back, wasn't that the same thing?

First time he'd run away was after Treveal Cliff; when his father had stopped him going out in Tom Stephens' boat, stopped him from going out with Jack. Treveal Cliff, that was the real first time, but no one ever knew, only Jack. Standback had felt so angry and betrayed by his father for forcing him to go and work just to please his little brother. He'd made up his mind to leave while he'd shivered out there on the cliff. He'd packed his duffel bag in the dark for fear of waking up the rest of the family. It was two o'clock in the morning; the sky was diamond bright with stars in the new moon. He'd set off over the meadow and up the hill to take the field path into Penzance. It was a clear night and the frost was already formed over the meadow. He jumped the granite stile, a flurry of disturbed wing and the coarse call of a pheasant came from deep in the hedge. His eyes became accustomed to the new moon darkness and he tramped on. He was still angry but the physical action of walking warmed him and the night air sights and sounds took him in a new direction.

There was a light in the window of Jack's little tin hut. It was the warm yellow glow of Jack's paraffin lamp. He felt he should say goodbye if Jack was still awake. He tapped softly, and Jack's face appeared across the stable door.

"Cześć," he said, as though it were normal to go visiting in the middle of the night. Then "Come, come in." He spoke softly. "Tread soft, see who else has come. You're not my first visitor tonight." He opened his big woollen coat to reveal a bundle of red fluff with two piercing golden eyes. "I found her tonight. Mr Blewett, he put out his snares, she is young and was caught. Now her leg is maybe broken. So I must be doctor and mother. I've been holding her close to me so that she will feel warm and secure."

It was not unusual for Jack to have a refugee in his home. Any creature, however large or small, was welcome in Jack's little tin shed. He'd rescued storm-tossed birds, bats; watched over butterflies that hibernated under his eaves, or the toad from the nearby hedge. Once a frog had become disoriented in snow, flopping around on its belly, the long frog legs unable to gain purchase as they sank in the soft April snow. Jack had taken it in his big palms and made a shelter out of wood and straw beneath his hut. Even beetles, earwigs and bees had found themselves wintering beneath the tin roof. No life was judged too meagre when it came to care.

"Did you see the seals?" Standback asked.

"They were having a great time in the waves, they were fishing, even if we weren't," Jack continued to speak softly.

"I'm leaving." It came out suddenly, and more emotionally than he'd expected. "I hate it here an' I hate Father, an' I'm goin'. I'm goin' tonight."

Jack nodded. "Where you go?" he asked.

"Work on the waltzers with Jim Stevens." It just came out again. He hadn't yet planned that far, but Jim always had money in his jacket pocket.

"Then, we must have drink to see you on your way," said Jack. He lay the young vixen very gently into a basket by the stove, and stroked its head. "We must help another stray," he whispered to the tiny creature. Then he stood up and took a bottle and two glasses from a shelf near a washing-up bowl. He poured clear liquid from the bottle into the glasses.

"Polish vodka very good for thinking, and this is very best Polish vodka," he said as he handed Standback the glass. "Na zdrowie!" said Jack, and swallowed the glass of vodka in one.

Standback did the same, and the fiery liquid burned his throat and warmed his chest.

"Now," Jack put two pillows down beside the stove, "sit, and tell me all that has occurred with you."

It had all poured out of him; and while he talked of the injustice of his Father's decision, the unfairness of having to work instead of going out on the boat; of his little brother's weedling, all the while Jack was listening and stroking the little vixen, calming it but still listening intently and whispering occasionally what had sounded like "Nie pwach . . . oo-spokuj sh-eh . . . lisku". He had asked for the Polish spelling. "Nie placz, unspokój się lisku." Jack kept repeating the words. It was hypnotic, the fire was flickering brightly in the cast-iron stove. It was warm by the stove, and the gentle stroking words and the warm vodka calmed him in the inside-outside smell of the little tin hut. He was enveloped, and felt safe while his anger turned to uncertainty and mourning for the child he was losing in his adolescent self. He was fourteen, he couldn't cry, he shouldn't cry, but he did cry, and Jack reached around his shoulders and drew him close into his big coat, into the musty scent of fox and the warmth of love.

"Synku mój," Jack said. "Synku mój, you are so lucky to have father," he paused. "I have father once and, like you, I would get cross with him. Is what sons and fathers must do. The son must test his strength against a safe opponent. You are lucky. I did not get that chance. Before I could fight with my father, I saw him dragged into the street outside our home in Warsaw where he was shot. My mother slapped me for crying. 'Be strong,' she said, 'Your father is hero.' . . . 'But why didn't he fight?' I cry . . . 'But he did fight,' said my mother. 'He stood and he faced their tyranny.' " And then Jack had explained how he and his mother had been taken to the camp in the cold north in Russia, where he had watched his mother die slowly from hard labour and starvation; and how they had survived by eating the rats.

"Stretch up and get that box, up there on the shelf," said Jack. Standback reached up and took down an intricately carved wooden box and handed it to Jack. "This box holds my history," said Jack.

"It's beautiful," Standback stared at the carving on the lid. "Flowers and Peacocks."

"Very Polish design." Jack opened the box. "All I have of my father is here, one tiny faded photograph in a wooden box, he and my mother too. I have also her little silver cross which she wore," he paused. "I would far rather have a head overflowing with memories of my parents as I grew into adulthood." Jack paused again. "You enjoy your father. Even when you disagree, the love is there, it never goes away. He loves you, I promise you," he said. "You must go back and give him gift."

"What?" he'd asked. "What gift can I give? I don't know what he'd like."

Jack thought, "Make him wycinanka! A father would be pleased to have some luck made by his son," he said.

For the next hour Jack had helped him to cut out a big paper doily, a 'vi-chinanka' in Jack's way of saying. It had taken ages to cut out all the tiny holes in the folded paper. The sky was turning pink as he'd made his way back to the house, the

70

precious paper gift in his pocket and his body warmed by love, the comfort of a small iron stove, and Polish vodka.

Matter do'a?

Standback stared at his brother. "Didden you never feel guilty?"

Eddie shrugged: "Cakeplate, Doily Jack! What's it matter? We was kids. Juss what we called him 'cos he didden speak like us an' we coulden say his name. I still can't. Jack Dash is easier say than Jan Whatscallums . . . juss . . ."

"Daszyński! Jan Daszyński!" he interrupted. "What's so hard about that? Thomas brothers said he stole their jobs, beat him up, broke his nose."

"We was kids, can't feel bad about that."

"You wasen there Eddie. I saw it happen."

"I seen the Thomas brothers fight often 'nuff."

"I was there!"

"So you was there. Why d'you want to bring that up now?"

"Why do you think?"

"Why do you do that?"

"What?"

"Answer questions with another question. You're so defensive."

Foreigners

He'd been fifteen when it happened, and Eddie six years younger. The Thomas brothers were wild. They always had been. They were twins. People tried to find reasons for their wildness, explanations for their behaviour, but they were just wild. Their father had left three nights after his wife had returned home with the lively and very vocal twin babies. Left

71

alone with her charges, Betty Thomas couldn't cope. She found ways to get through, normally a bottle, but occasionally a reefer and later, when her boys were fully grown and challenging, black bombers. Meanwhile her boys found their own way.

Nick Thomas, the elder by 3 minutes, famously challenged the leader of the local chapter of Hell's Angels. The story was legend. Bandit, the leader of the Angels, bet Nick would be chicken on the back of his Triumph Bonneville doing a ton. Nick Thomas had never ridden a motorbike but he loved a challenge and needed a lift back home to West Penwith after a good night out in St. Austell, so he accepted the bet. Nick stared at the road over Bandit's shoulder, and when he'd seen the speedometer coming up through 90 to 95, he flung his hands across Bandit's visor. The Bonny wobbled and Nick shouted in Bandit's ear, "Juss keep her goin'. I'll tell ee when to stop." That's what the Thomas boys were like. They didn't like Doily Jack, he was a POW is what they said; well a few people got the European Volunteer Workers confused with Prisoners of War; and anyone with a foreign accent didn't fit, not so far as the Thomas brothers were concerned. Any accent north of Penwith was foreign if they felt like it, and Polish was German to their ears.

What Grandad said to Tourists:
"You can't start from here!"

Grandad had been full of tales. Sometimes his tales were tales he made up to illustrate his own take on life, his own philosophy. Sometimes he'd marry a story he'd heard with a bit of home-grown wisdom. He was not above stealing other people's tales and making them his own experience. It was just what Grandad did.

Eddie had told Grandad's story so often that now he often told it as his own.

"Well I was up top of the lane one time, leanin' on the stand where the milk churns used to be, when up come this posh young couple in a brand new Jaguar. 'I say,' says the young man, 'Can you possibly tell us how to get to Zennor?' Well he was facing St. Ives so he must've driven straight past Zennor. So I says to him, 'You can't start from here,' an' he's lookin' at me, all bemused. 'So where can we start from?' says his missus, all hoity-toity like. 'Well,' I says, 'If I was you I'd carry on up along the next right, up there where it d'say Towednack, an' you can turn round there. Then you can start from there. Come back down by 'ere, but don't stop 'ere, carry on up the hill an' go round the big bend there, then up the hill past Eagle's Nest . . . thass the name of the house up there on the carn. Pass there, then down, round another bend and on, and another bend and down a bit more an' he's the turning there, on the right, that'll take you into Zennor."

"Why can't I juss turn round here?" asks the driver.

"You do that an' you'll take the sump off that posh car of yours. Back in 'ere an' she'll belly down on the grass, see. Mind, you woulden be the furst, bit of a sharp incline."

1972

It seemed to Standback that everything had gone wrong in the nineteen-seventies. In fact, during the many times he had considered it, it seemed that 1972 in particular could be pinpointed as the beginning of the end of a security in life which he had known since childhood. In 1972 he had been safe in the knowledge that he was born on a farm that belonged to his father and to his grandfather before that. The Hosken family had farmed through four generations. Nobody had ever been rich, but neither had anyone ever really starved. The farm had produced a livelihood; enough to feed each of the

73

generations. Farming was in the blood. The land would provide. It had only been a small farm, what they used to call a mixed farm. Grandad had been one of eight children, it might have been ten if the other two hadn't been still-born. So there had been times when sons went to the mines, some went to fishing, and daughters went into service, or married out of the farm, more often than not though, they'd married into another farm.

He'd known throughout his childhood that, like his father before him, he would eventually take over Trevarnon, or maybe he and Eddie would run it together. It was not uncommon for sons to take joint ownership. Trevarnon had provided for his mother and father, his brother and himself as well as Granma and Grandad and Uncle Jack. If they hadn't sold the cliff fields over to the National Trust, if . . . he wrestled with the tangle of thoughts in his head.

For a long time he had searched his mind for something to blame for what had happened. It was his father's fault for selling the cliff fields to the National Trust and then dying; it was Uncle Jack's fault for leaving; his mother's fault for being so ill for so long; Eddie's fault for giving up on the farm and going mining; Eddie's wife Christine's fault for wanting a built-in bathroom and all the luxuries that a Geevor wage packet provided. For years he had sought for the cause, for the moment, the exact action, the precise moment in time when the line of the Hoskens had broken. The line that had gone back through Father, Grandad, and all the Hoskens for generations. Why had the line broken with him? He had wrestled with his anger, and then with his guilt. He'd got drunk, and then he'd run away.

Something Changed in the 1970s – i

War can cause change, so can famine, flood and disease. These are big things that you notice, you experience the change, you know what started it. But change can happen in many small things, things which are not immediately connected, and that is the sort of change that you don't see happening, you just wake up one day to find yourself not quite recognising the world around you.

In the 1950s milk was delivered to your door, and the post arrived in the morning. There were changes happening but they seemed to happen gradually, the arrival of mains water was gradual, the arrival of mains electricity was gradual. If you wanted to telephone you would more than likely go to find a red telephone box, few people had a telephone in their home. There were village shops, village post offices, village garages and going to town was an event. There would be deliveries by van: the butcher, the bread van, the fishmonger and the grocer. You would go to Penzance for Market Day, Corpus Christi Fair, or if you needed to visit the bank, or the dentist or doctor, or needed to buy a new suit or winter coat and hat, or shoes; or go to the cinema or a dance.

The arrival of the railway in Penzance at the end of the nineteenth-century had been a big change. It took the flowers and fish freshly to London markets and it brought the curious visitors to the Cornish Riviera. There were coaches by road, and coastal steamships. Then the arrival of the motor car, one or two at first, so noteworthy that you'd run out to look at them. Gradually the trains and cars brought even more visitors, and they came to stay on campsites at farms, at hotels and guest houses, and a new industry of visitors was developing.

There had been a Woolworth's in Penzance, Wilton & Nicholls, General Ironmongers, and a Wimpy Bar. The arrival of Tesco to Penzance was a big change; Tesco and the beginning of self-service shopping. For most of his early life, there had been corner shops in Penzance. It had been that way for ever it had seemed to him. Grandad had talked the same way about saddlers and blacksmiths and wells, but none of that had meant anything until the nineteen-seventies. That was when he had begun to feel like a foreigner in his own clothes, only he hadn't understood why, not then. He only understood now that he had returned. Now he could see that his world, the old world, lay beneath the present, and it made the new world familiar and strange at the same time.

Deluge

He likened it to watching the rain fall in the yard after a perfect bright and sunny morning. You'd feel the wind change and the first few drops of rain would fall with space between them, a space long enough to watch the dry mud dance in little clouds. Within minutes the rain would fall heavily and the ground was too wet to make little clouds. That was how the seventies had brought change, in a deluge.

First it was decimalisation; later the M5 motorway reached all the way to Exeter. The M5 brought more people than the train. The toll on the Tamar Bridge was paid with the new decimal coins; and the people loved the Cornish countryside and they found farmhouses for sale for five thousand pounds and they relocated. In the mid-1960s Westward Television had made a film which celebrated the amount of industry relocating in the south-west.

But in 1972 the coal miners went on strike for the first time in fifty years and the Government declared a State of Emergency. This, he felt, was the start of the biggest deluge. The Common Market, the European Economic Community, fish quotas, milk quotas. Little had his father realised what was happening to the farms. Supermarkets offered fruits and vegetables all year round, whatever the growing season in the UK. Brazil nuts and Mandarin oranges were no longer just for Christmas. The supermarket shelves heaved with goods and 'choice' became the buzz word of the food economy. Without knowing it people began to eat more bacon from Denmark, not Billy Blewett's dad's pigs in the arcs. In fact, they didn't even notice that the arcs were empty.

What Grandad Said

"Cornish hedge is like your mother's thread, holds everythin' together. Work of art. Thass why you got to learn to look. Once you pick up a stone you got to use it. Never pick a stone up twice."

Maybe that's what they had to do. Just as their mother had darned the farm overalls, patched the knees and elbows where the fabric had worn threadbare. Now they must mend the hedges to hold the land together.

Wycinanki

Standback looked up and across the hedge towards his brother. Eddie's head was down as he concentrated on his work. Suddenly Eddie looked up to see that Standback was staring at him. Standback nodded to his brother, then bent again towards the stones.

"Fancy that pasty now?" Eddie asked.

Eddie produced his flask and two large steak pasties

77

wrapped in paper bags. He handed one of the bags to his brother, "Philps," he said, "Large."

Standback accepted the pasty. "Cheers," he said.

The early spring sunshine felt warm. All morning Standback had been working in the chill of the wind on the eastern side of the hedge, but the sun had warmed the western side and he hunkered down against the warm granite stones. Rock made from fire held the fire. Eddie sat down a little further along, keeping the slender distance between them. He was reading a newspaper. Standback pulled the pasty half out of its bag. Holding it by the bag he took a bite and chewed slowly. He hadn't had a decent pasty for a long time. They ate in silence. He still wasn't happy that Eddie had felt so confident of his coming to work with him that he'd brought two pasties and a flask of tea.

When he'd finished eating, Standback slipped his cap down over his eyes and folded his arms as if resting. From under his cap he watched Eddie as he read his paper. He wasn't sure that Eddie's arm was quite so bad as he'd said. He'd managed to work pretty well for a one-armed man.

Eddie put down the newspaper he'd been reading so that he could hold the flask between his knees in order to unscrew the top. He felt Standback watching and he looked up.

"Fancy a beer?" He said, as he put down his flask. "Got a couple cans in the rucksack."

Eddie really had come prepared. Standback leaned across to take the can. "Mind if I look at the paper?" He asked. He reached inside his pocket for his pen-knife as he spoke.

"Suit yourself," said Eddie.

Eddie was strangely confident, and so prepared. Everything about Eddie confused Standback. Eddie cared about hedging, he cared about what was happening in Cornwall, he cared enough about his brother to bring food, tea and even beer, so why did he feel so uneasy in Eddie's company?

He took out the properties section from *The Cornishman*, and with the scissors of his Swiss army knife he cut off a single page and made a square from the corner. Then he folded the square diagonally, first one way and then the other. With his thumb nail he sharpened the edges. With the scissor blade of his Swiss army knife he began to cut V-shapes along the folds.

"I haven't finished readin' that!" Eddie stared at him. "You idden making doilies?"

"Wycinanki." He repeated the word slowly with the pronunciation taught to him by Jack, "Vi-chi-nanki. Vi-chi-nanka for juss one." He said it carefully to get it right. It was years since he had tried his tongue around the foreign words. "It's a Polish traditional craft, made for special occasions. Birthdays, deaths, weddin's an' all, though they don't have birthdays, not like we do. They call it Name Day, bit like our Saint's Day, Jack said."

"Christ almighty! He'd have they doilies hanging over the door of that tin shed of his every bleddy chance he got! Embarrassin' it was. They took the piss out of me at school. 'What's Cakeplate celebratin' today?' "

Standback looked at his brother. "Did you always think of Jack as . . . you know, diff'rent?"

"Well he was, everyone knaw that."

"It didn't matter though, not really, him being Polish. I mean there were Polish men down Geevor."

"Course. But you can't say they belong here. Your birthplace is who you are. Where you belong to be."

"You belong to be up Truro then," said Standback.

"Don't be bleddy ridic'lus!"

79

"Course I was born 'ere, right 'ere! On this land." Standback grinned.

They'd reached yet another impasse.

"Jack finished up walkin' the lanes. Never knew what made him leave. I mean what made him go when he did?" Eddie asked.

Standback didn't know how to answer.

Walking the Lanes

It had always seemed to Standback that taking to the lanes would have been a good thing to do.

Happy Harry had lived in the lanes, he'd heard his father and grandfather talk about Harry. An old tramp they'd said. Only felt safe in the open air. Others just said he was feral, or simple. He'd found out later that Harry used to go around and sing to get money. It was said that he'd originally come from a well-to-do family. It was said his two brothers turned up one day to try to persuade him to go back home, but he wouldn't go. He'd stay in a place for a while, sing for coppers and then move on. He preferred to wander in the open air. Grandad said that Mr Butters from the bakery used to leave him buns and pasties at the edge of the places where he stayed when he was down Boscaswell. He visited all over, some said up Sancreed and over Zennor. They said that Harry roamed about Penwith. Grandad'd come in some nights and say, "Happy Harry's home. Seen his light in the hedge." Harry hadn't been the only one to use a hedge as shelter; in the old days miners sometimes used to rest in the thickets rather than walk six miles home and six miles back to the mine between shifts.

What Grandad said about the Lanes

Grandad had lots of tales about poverty. Grandad could remember the Workhouse at Madron Village. *"I'd sooner walk the lanes,"* he'd say *"than go in there."* Grandad's Aunty Lizbeth lived in Madron and one Christmas Grandad got sent over to his Aunty's house to help out because his Uncle Stephen had broken his arm. Uncle Stephen was a Blacksmith. *"I'll never forget that Christmas,"* Grandad said. *"It was horrible, I was still a boy really, only juss thirteen an' I had to do a man's work alright. But I'll never forget that Christmas, the sound of they clogs when the poor orphans scraped along the road to worship of a Sunday. They poor orphans, their faces was haunted, some of 'em wasn't even orphans; but you didden stay together up the Poor House. Husbands and wives separated, kids separated from their parents, an' all for bein' poor. Tes only a harvest away . . . make me shudder to remember. I'd sooner walk the lanes any day."*

People didn't walk the lanes these days thought Standback. These days they stayed in town and sat in doorways. It was still poverty.

Battleground

As kids they'd called it Witches Rock because years before that's what it had been called. Some people said it was where they used to burn the witches; and they called the moorland Burn Down. Billy Blewett reckoned that it was all nonsense and the name 'Burn' only came from the fact that his dad used to periodically burn the bracken off the hill. Hill fires had always happened, either controlled fires for clearing bracken and undergrowth or uncontrolled fires caused by careless visitors; campers who didn't know how to put out a fire properly, or passers-by who threw lighted cigarettes into the dry furze. The furze which used to be collected as fuel for cottage fires. The furze which Jack Dash used to light his cast-iron stove in the little green hut. A hill fire could travel underground along the roots of gorse.

Witches Rock stuck with the pupils of the local village school. It became the place where you dealt with those who posed a danger to you. Cakeplate was dangerous, he was different. It wasn't a conscious, considered difference, it was borrowed from the goodies and baddies in Westerns, and detective and war films; storybook villains, wicked witches, the Sheriff of Nottingham, the enemy. The Germans had become the real enemy; but it all began with stories and became re-played to mean any people not like us, people better off, people misunderstood. The Tigs brothers were ostracised in primary school because they were gippos and lived in a caravan. June and Stan Connor were different because they were devout Catholics and had a separate assembly when it came to secondary school. Cakeplate had a separate assembly as well. Just being different was enough. Cakeplate was the most different. He was Polish, a European Volunteer Worker, not that that meant anything to the kids at school. As Eddie said, 'Jan Daszyńksi, who can say the name? Thass why we call him Jack Dash.' Standback called him Uncle Jack. Eddie called him Cakeplate at school, and Jack at home.

There was a Polish community outside Newquay, up St. Mawgan. Jack said it wasn't as big as some camps. Cakeplate lived at Trevarnon Farm, in the little green tin hut. Jan Daszyński was his real name, and even that wasn't his real name, however hard he'd tried to learn to pronounce it, it was not the way Jan would have spoken it in his own tongue.

Jack had told him all about the wycinanki, how his grandma

had taught him how to cut them out, how the paper patterns might celebrate life and luck. He had also said that in the years before glass was used in windows, the people had used animal hides to keep out the cold, and that they used to cut tiny holes in the hides in order to let in the light during the cold winter months.

Many plans were hatched on Battleground; in the end it didn't happen there.

Corpus Christi

The fair came into Penzance for Corpus Christi. Princess May Recreation Ground would be covered by stalls, coconut shies, and often a boxing tent; as well as the rides, the Big Wheel, the Dodgems, Waltzers, Hall of Mirrors, Wall of Death, and a Ghost Train. All the way up Tolver Road were cheap-jacks, selling boxes of crockery, sets of saucepans, fluffy animals and giant plastic hammers. The lights screamed in the darkness of night, screams hung out of the chairs on the Big Wheel, and bounced off the Wall of Death. Sirens screeched through the popular music from some of the rides; and the dim lights of the cheap-jacks disguised the logos on products. It was a magical transformation of normality. Girls dressed up and leaned on their partners' arms. Boys paraded in their drape jackets, then leather jackets, whatever the fashion of the day. The pubs did well and there was an air of excitement in the fumes and rumble from the generators. The Thomas Brothers worked the waltzers. Their reputation preceded them. In their drainpipe jeans, slicked hair and leather jackets they flung their power as they spun the chairs. To the innocent girls in the chairs they were romantic devils, enticing and challenging. Their own local Marlon Brando or James Dean, boys turned bad through circumstance; and the Thomas boys knew how to play their roles.

As a fifteen year old Cornish boy Standback had marvelled at this new breed of teenager and, along with his mates, he had emulated the look at least. They'd wandered slowly up the street of stalls, watched as the cheap-jacks worked their magic, and hung around the rides, leaning against safety barriers, thumbs hooked under their belts. Local doctors prepared for the annual rise in pregnancies.

Corpus Christi : The trucks

Corpus Christi was a big event in Penzance. Whitelegs Fair came to town. The big trucks would crawl into lay-bys and queue along the side of the road all the way from Ludgvan Leaze to Three Tunnels. They would wait for church services to be over on Sunday before they crawled into town, heavy with the promise of excitement and unreality. Jim Stevens' father owned a pub in town and old Man Stevens had made a deal with Mr Whitelegs. If his boy Jim went out and put a crate of Guinness onto the back of his truck as it went through Market Jew Street, Mr Whitelegs would throw out a wad of free tickets. Jim managed manfully, the big truck was slow-moving and as it crawled majestically up the gradient towards Market House and Humphry Davy's statue, Jim jumped aboard the running-board of the truck, left the crate of Guinness, and was duly rewarded with a handful of tickets that would make him everyone's best friend for the whole of Corpus Christi week.

The Fair built in intensity during the week as the big rides opened and the music swelled towards the crescendo of Saturday Night, the last night. On Saturday night, the music started early as the rides and stalls came to life. The loud music in the daytime closed all the open windows of the houses in Penzance, as if for fear the temporary excesses and wickedness of the fairground might float into the sleepy bedroom windows of innocents and infect them with a lust for the travelling life.

Corpus Christi: Witness

The Hosken boys were beneficiaries of Jim Stevens' tickets and Standback took his younger brother to the fair. They got off the bus at the top of Causewayhead and walked along towards the whistles and music of the fairground. As always the road up to Princess May Recreation Ground, where the fair was held, was lined with cheap-jacks. "Royal Doulton dinner sets! Going for a song! Dinner for six! Just for tonight. Not five pounds, not four pounds, not three pounds; look at it, dinner plates, side plates, what you gonna give me, not five, not four, not three, thirty bob, to the first four sold . . ."

Then the hands shot up and the pre-packed boxes were exchanged for the cash and the customers left. Sometimes, some of the plates at the bottom of the box were cracked, even broken. Sometimes, it was obvious they were seconds, faulty from the moment they came off the factory line. No one liked to admit they'd been had, and despite the fault they were a bargain none the less, and anyway, how often did you have six to dinner?

Children ran amongst the crowds. No one worried, they'd be met at the waltzers, behind the dodgems, under the big wheel; and the children ran wild to discover the strange unreality of the fair which screamed loudly with cries, music and shouting. It was dangerous and dreamlike. It was a world where anything might happen; a world that smelled of sweet candy-floss, toffee apples, hot-dogs, hair-spray, fear and excitement.

They'd done the waltzers and the rifle range. Standback had shot three ducks. Then, on their way to the big wheel, Eddie wanted to go on the dodgems. While he waited with his brother, Standback saw the Thomas brothers pass by on the other side of the dodgem ride. They were strutting and laughing, and a crowd of other boys followed the Thomas brothers and they disappeared from Standback's sight, round behind the ghost train towards a hot-dog stall. The dodgems were filling slowly; Standback pressed the money into Eddie's hand, "I'll be back afore it's finished," he said, and he followed after the crowd of boys. He sensed something about to go off. Looked like a fight, there was always at least one fight at the fair.

Standback caught up with the small crowd of youths as they circled and he could hear voices coming from the centre. He elbowed through and saw that Jack was being served at the hot-dog stall. He hadn't seen Jack for almost a year, not since Jack had taken to the lanes. As Jack took a hot-dog and handed over the money to the stall holder, Nick Thomas pushed into his back. Jack dropped the money, it scattered onto the muddy grass. Jack ignored Nick, as though it had been an accident, and bent down to retrieve his money. He stood up and finished paying. Then, still grasping the hot-dog, he turned to make his way out of the circle, but it closed in behind him, between Jack and the hot-dog stall. Each time Jack turned away, Nick Thomas stood directly in front of him, barring his exit.

"You idden wanted 'ere, Cakeplate!" Nick Thomas jeered. "We don't want no Germans takin' our jobs do us?" he turned and shouted out to the general crowd. Jack made to walk around Nick, but Dave Thomas stepped forward and stood next to his twin, forcing Jack to step backwards.

"He don't understand," shouted Nick to his audience. "Want us to *sprechen ze Deutsch*, do 'ee, German?"

The crowd roared with laughter as Nick marched around Jack in imaginary jackboots, his right arm in a Nazi salute.

"I am a Polish national," said Jack, turning to face Nick. "I am no friend to the Germans."

As Jack turned again to walk away from the Thomas brothers. Nick grabbed his jacket and pushed him. Standback ran into the circle

"It's the truth!" he'd shouted. "Jack idden no German! He used to work for us up the farm." He stood ready to fight, he'd had a couple of fights at school with classmates.

"No, stay back," Jack had said.

"Thass right," said Dave Thomas, "stand back, Standback!" He sneered. The crowd laughed loudly.

Standback's heart had been pounding but he was ready to fight. He was ready to go in. At that moment Nick threw a punch that broke Jack's nose but Jack still didn't fight back. He'd moved, so that the next two blows missed him, but then he'd walked straight into Dave Thomas's right hand and the hot-dog flew into the mud. The crowd laughed. Standback remembered how ashamed he'd felt. He'd seen the way Jack lifted bales, he knew that Jack was stronger than Nick Thomas and Dave Thomas, but Jack just wouldn't hit back.

"Coward!" shouted Nick.

"Coward! Coward!" chanted the crowd of boys. Three times Nick Thomas knocked Jack to the ground to the cheers of the crowd; and three times Jack had stood up but he wouldn't fight back. Then someone said the police were coming. The Thomas brothers bolted and the crowd evaporated.

Jack held a handkerchief against his bleeding nose. "Sorry you had to see that," he'd said to Standback.

Standback had been angry; "Why'd you let 'em do it? Why didden you hit back?"

Jack had reached out to put his arm around Standback's shoulder but he'd shrugged him off.

"Why'd you let him make a fool of you? You could beat Nick Thomas any time. You're stronger than Nick Thomas," he'd shouted.

"That is why I must not hit back," Jack had said, and he was wincing as he spoke because of a cut on his lip.

"But you could have beaten them easy."

"I could have killed them," said Jack.

"Then why didn't you?"

"That is not my way," said Jack.

Jack had seen that Standback was ashamed. "You'll understand one day," he'd said, but Standback had never understood. He'd turned on his heels and left, turning back he shouted:

"Coward! *Coward!*"

Not until long after Jack had died did he begin to think about it all over again. There were lots of things he hadn't understood about Jack. Had he upset him that night when he'd run away to Jack's hut? It wasn't long after that winter night that Jack had taken to the lanes. He'd seen him once or twice afterwards but their relationship seemed changed. Jack became more distant, a stranger to him. Jack had survived in much the same way as Billy Blewett had survived, only different times. He'd sharpened tools and knives, mended pots, been a handyman, and lived off the land. Even in the eighties people still wanted their knives sharpened and pots mended. All the same, when he thought of Jack nowadays he felt so guilty. They'd found Jack lying on a camp bed in a chalet in woods below the hill, not all that far away from the farm, less than ten miles. Turned out that Grandad had got him a job with one of his old farming friends who was running a chalet site. Jack got a chalet in return for being a caretaker and odd-job man. Jack had died of a heart attack in his sleep they'd said. Just like Billy, that's probably why it had all come back so strongly. He'd missed Jack's funeral because he'd arrived drunk and couldn't remember anything. He'd made sure he didn't drink at Billy's funeral. He felt so guilty about Jack. He'd never had the opportunity to tell him that he did understand why he hadn't fought back. He understood because he had discovered the same dark strength in himself.

Vertical Meadows

At some point between the flowering of the blackthorn and the flowering of the hawthorn, the hedges look their best. This is when they look new, not yet burnt by the wind; although the thorn trees will always point the way of the prevailing winds. The greens are brilliant and fresh, not yet layered in the dust from traffic. In May the cow parsley is still upright and lacy, the campions stand to attention, the bracken is still young and tender and not yet all consuming. By Spring Bank Holiday, the parchment-brown remains of last year's ferns have almost overnight sprung into viridian spikes. The grasses and sedges are as elegant as cultivated ornamental plants. There are still bluebells, and the majestic foxgloves are just about to bloom. There are constellations of pink herb robert and indigo twinkles of speedwell. On a cool misty morning, the sunlight turns the webs of spiders into necklaces of diamonds glinting on the hedges. At dawn the hedges brim over with the song of birds, as they do again at sunset as the birds settle to roost. On quiet nights you can sit and listen to all the rustling and squeaking of life, and it's a special treat to hear the gorse popping as it blossoms on a rare still spring or autumn day. If you are very lucky you might even see the honey bees swarm along the hedge-line. It is then that you know you are in the land of milk and honey.

It is estimated by the Guild of Cornish Hedgers, who support and maintain the ancient craft of hedging, that Cornwall's hedges add up to a wildlife area of roughly 50,000 acres, and contain around 600 flowering species. There are woody species, as well as the grasses, sedges, ferns, lichens and mosses. A mile of Cornish hedge should typically contain between two to three hundred plant species say the Guild. The Guild have diligently researched and monitored stretches of hedgerow. The plants attract insects which in turn bring the other creatures: the mammals, reptiles and birds who feed from, and live in, the habitat. Some creatures prefer the darker side of the hedge, the damp crevices between the stones suits the toad; others prefer the side which faces the sun. Some build their homes in the trees which grow in the hedges: hawthorn, blackthorn, honeysuckle, ivy, and dog roses. Others nestle between the roots of plants and in crevices, with the violet, bluebell, common vetch and wood avens. The more you look, the more you will see. Butterflies, honey bees, bumble bees, beetles, moths, they all benefit from the hedges. Indeed everything, including man, benefits from the hedges.

A Man Called Father

Standback unfolded the paper wycinanka carefully, and held it up so that the sunlight filtered through the tiny holes he had cut out. "Mother said Uncle Jack's used to be like filigree lace. I remember one Christmas we had 'em up in the house, on the mantelpiece."

His brother stared at him. "Jack never went in the house.

Granma woulden let him, said he was feral. Thass why he lived up the hut."

"Was before you was born, Eddie. When Father come home after the war."

He could still feel his three-year-old anticipation and excitement. At last he was to meet the man called 'Father'.

Father was the smiling black-haired man in uniform who looked out from a photograph on the mantelpiece. Father was the man who had been 'missing at sea' and Father was dead. Sometimes his mother talked about his father with Granma and Grandad. They would talk with sad voices. Being dead was a sad thing, like when the kitten had drowned in the water butt when it fell off the roof; but Standback hadn't felt sad because nothing had changed for him. He'd played with the kitten, but he'd never even met his father. One day when he was three, a telegram arrived at the farmhouse and everyone was crying because Father was no longer dead. Granma had said, "What about the boy? What about Benjamin?" He remembered how he'd felt when his mother had beckoned him close, "It looks as though your father might be coming home after all," she'd said, and her shoulders shook as she'd held him a little too tightly.

After being missing at sea, his father had been rescued by fishermen but he'd lost his memory. He'd ended up in a German prison camp and then in a British military hospital. But now he could remember again and was coming home for Christmas.

His three-year-old self hadn't really understood what any of the details meant but he was beside himself with excitement. It was going to be the best Christmas ever. His father was coming home. The big smiling man in the photograph would walk through the door proudly and pick up his son and hug him. Only the man who came through the door didn't look like the man on the mantelpiece. The man who came through the door was old and thin; and his eyes weren't smiling, they looked empty and defeated. He'd run up to the man called Father who looked shocked and pushed him away. It had been the first time they had met, and his father had pushed him away.

"It was like he didden see me, Eddie."

"Must've been hard for him. Woulden've even known he had a son, I don't s'pose."

He stared blankly at Eddie. "I don't think he ever really saw me."

"Diff'rant generation. Wasn't brought up to wear his heart on his sleeve. He taught us everything, everything we know, took us rugby on a Saturday, bottle of pop, bar of dairy milk."

"I coulden never reach the man."

"You coulden! I coulden never get past you!"

Standback stared at his brother. He couldn't breathe. He turned towards the cliff.

"Where you going?" Eddie asked.

"Need some air, head's boilin'."

Eddie's words rang after him. "Thass it! Run away! What you allus do! What you do best! . . . Standback!"

What Grandad said about Human Nature:

"Big things happen and you think you'll never get used to the change, and pretty soon you can't remember how it was before: like when they rearrange the supermarket shelving. Kept coming home without tea-bags: now I can't remember what it used to be like. Or the remote control on the TV, took me ages to stop gettin' up to switch channels, or when they change the design of somethin' you allus buy an' you don't recognise it no more an' you can't remember what it's called 'cos you recognise it by the picture. Even Big things like death, tes all the same really, life, death, milk quotas, industrial

92

farming, aeroplanes. Life changes, an' you juss get used to it an' forget what you had before. You juss have to carry on.

Granma used to say she looked forward to the Spring 'cos everything do come back, all the leaves come back an' the grass an' primroses an' all. I tole her, they leaves aven't come back, they're new leaves, and them flowers is new flowers, the old leaves an' flowers 'ave to die so the new ones can come, juss like us. Granma, she didden like see things that way, but I do. Life an' death. Tes a continuum."

The Granite Mirror

It had been a mistake to come back to Cornwall. It laid bare all the old hurt. He didn't know how to express himself. Eddie didn't have dark days or dark thoughts; or if he did, he dismissed them. Eddie saw the good in things, even misfortune. Eddie didn't let things worry him for long. He had a way of rationalising everything. That was a good thing. Standback wished he could be the same, but he couldn't. He'd hoped that by coming back to Trevarnon today he could leave behind the black thoughts, but meeting up with Eddie seemed only to accentuate the darkness within him.

Each step towards the ocean seemed to cleanse his brain. He slid down through the thicket wood, which was a field of snowdrops in late January, early February. Leaving the wood, he continued along the path that followed the river into the cove. The blackthorn branches stung his bare arms. The river, down to his right, ran fast and fierce as it rushed to the sea; it sang in his ears. Then he was walking away from the moss and the water and the cool, and up the pathway towards the promontory that looked straight out onto Seal Island. He charged on. Yet again, it was all the same but somehow different. The path was well cut out, something they used to do themselves, always keeping it a little bit rough so that it wasn't too attractive to visitors. He crossed the rock where the adders basked in summer and came upon a brand new stile. There was a sign which said: "Please close the gate. Cattle roaming the cliffs." There had never been a gate in the past. It irked him; unlike his brother, he couldn't accept the change. Of course change happened but he hadn't been part of this. It had been done to him.

He met the coastal path and saw that on the flat stone where they had played lighthouse as kids, someone had put a bench. Somehow such a domestic thing looked wrong on the wild Atlantic cliff. He carried on, ignoring a warning sign that tried to redirect him from the old footpath due to 'unsafe cliffs'. He descended the 'unsafe cliffs', their boyhood route into the cove. He clung to the grass, as they'd done as kids, putting his feet one in front of the other on the steep narrow incline into the cove until he reached the rocks, where they used to pile up driftwood to take up to the farm.

He looked out to Seal Island and saw the grey-black head in the frothy waters. Barely stopping, he turned left to cross the rocks into the next gully. There was a nest of boulders that spilled out from the cliff over a natural pool where, as a boy, he would sit and stare out to sea. Beyond Seal Island the next land mass was America. It seemed like looking into the stars, an impossibly unreal distance.

He had never intended to come all the way to the cove, though Eddie would never believe him. He'd only intended to get to the cliff-top and stare out over the sea before going back. He hadn't intended to come down to the pool but now that he was here, he knew he was in the right place.

The sea spray splashed over his boots. He took them off, rolled up his jeans and went down onto a rocky shelf in the water of Cap'n Billy's pool. Barking like a dog, he was gratified to see the grey-black head of a seal bob up from the waves just a couple of yards from where he stood knee-deep in the surf. Seals always came to the sound of barking, or singing. The big seal eyes stared at the foreign fish in its waters. The eyes seemed to see right into his soul. The seal held him in its gaze, it seemed to be examining him closely. He stood still and stared back, then it barked and slid down beneath the water surface. The tide was coming in and the waves were crashing against the rocks of Cap'n Billy's Pool. It was not a good time to be on this shelf for the tide would come in fast now and the water would soon be boiling and frothing, making the pool dangerous. He heaved himself out and sat in the nook of rocks he'd sat in years before. From here he could sit like a king on a throne and watch the water rising. His new-found friend surfaced again in the waves, rolled over and the deep soul-filled eyes still stared up at him. As a child he had thought that seals were the souls of drowned dogs. It always seemed to him that they were ancient beings. They could be playful, they could give you a harsh knock under water if you didn't respect their wildness, but they also had deep wisdom. He found himself speaking out loud, "You know what it's all about, don't you?" The seal rolled belly up, flopped its tail on the water and then raised its head just above the waves and barked. The soulful eyes seemed to embrace him. He could lose himself in its stare, then the spell broke as the seal barked in a way that sounded like laughter. And then it dived, and this time it swam back out to the island, back to its own world. He heard himself speak out loud, "Sometimes I can't face the granite," he said. He felt lonely without the seal's presence, but he also felt calm. He remained sitting, and stared out at the granite rocks as the night of Jack's funeral came back to him with his father's voice.

"Tes the granite, tes hard see, the granite mirror. Lot of people can't take it. They come down 'ere to escape, come to get away from it all, start a new life . . . it don't last, can't escape from yourself can'ee? Granite's hard, the granite mirror reflects back at you. Makes you face yourself. They can't take it. Jack could, but he was eaten up inside by the war. Thass why he took to the lanes. The war did terrible things to people."

He remembered being aware that his father was trying to tell him something, but he'd been drinking so much back then and it was all confused, all he'd ever remembered was his anger and bitterness about the land sale to the National Trust. Arguing about losing the farm had felt normal and it had drowned out the doctor's voice saying, "Your father has cancer, Mr Hosken, but he's not going to die tomorrow. He could have four good years left yet."

A cloud of black flies hung above some weed and a plastic container on the rocks nearby. He watched the circling black cloud idly. There were also lots of flies on the plastic bottle but none of them were moving, they appeared to be stuck to the plastic. He remembered how the windscreen of the car used to be covered in the blood and bodies of flies and other insects after a long drive. He'd always had the job of washing the windscreen and scraping off the mashed wings and bodies glued to the glass in their own blood. Sometimes he could only get them off by scraping his thumbnail against them. He remembered chasing Eddie with his bloody fingernails. Every Sunday he had to clean the car windscreen. He got to hate the flies. It was war, and there were always thousands more flies to come and be smashed on the glass. A wave funnelled up the rocks and the plastic container rolled,

96

'Poison' it said on the underside. Nowadays he never had to clean the flies from the windscreen and it scared him to wonder about their absence.

He remained seated for a while before he climbed back over the rocks and up the path, he felt calmer now. It struck him for the first time that Jack's funeral had been the closest his father had ever got to talking about the war. He'd never talked about his loss of memory, or his time in the German prison camp, none of it; but that night in the North Inn, at Jack's funeral, he'd opened up, just a tiny bit. He tried again to remember more of what his father had said. He'd tried so often, but what with the booze and his anger, whatever they'd talked about was lost. However, as he stared at the water it struck him that both he and his father had been angry, they'd both needed to let out the anger and neither of them had been able to speak about dying and the moment they had shared together in the hospital, the moment which had happened only a week before Jack's funeral, the moment when his father's diagnosis of cancer had been confirmed.

He watched a black-back gull circle slowly overhead and he listened to the rolling pebbles as each wave sucked away before crashing in again, breaking in splinters of silver spray against the black rocks. How he'd missed that sound. The powerful sound of the restless Atlantic Ocean fighting the granite.

The Tides of Life: The Find

Eddie slid a stone from the pile and set it into the last gap on the row. His brother's disappearance annoyed him but he had been pleasantly surprised at how easily they had been able to work together when they put their minds to it. They knew each other's ways. Eddie hadn't had such satisfaction working on a

e

hedge for years. He went over to the pile of rab and dug in with his shovel. He hit something in the earth. Something bulky, but not stone, was wrapped in rotting sackcloth. He hadn't noticed it when he'd piled up the fill in preparation for the repair. The earth had come out in hard clumps, held together with roots and age. Now that the roots had dried out in the open air the earth had loosened and fallen from the sacking cover. Eddie brushed aside the sacking and earth from a wooden box. It had once been beautifully and intricately carved with flower and bird shapes, the remains of lacquer flaking off in the sudden fresh air. He went to open the box and then hesitated. He looked over towards the cliff, there was no sign yet of his brother's return. He opened the box.

Secrets & Lies – ii

Eddie stared at the photograph, it was old and faint. It was a picture of a couple with a baby. They were standing in front of a green tin hut which had doilies hanging over the door. He was reaching into his jacket pocket for his glasses when he heard Standback whistling. He shoved the photograph into his sling and stood up hurriedly, the box fell from his lap, fell back into the pile of fill in which he'd found it. He scuffed loose earth over the top of the box to cover it.

"Lookin' good!" Standback said as he stared at the hedge. "Like you say, want a hedge built or mended, get in the Hosken boys." Eddie barely looked up from his work. Standback had expected a slagging off for being gone for so long. "Sooner you get that sling off the better," he paused; "Still hurt do'a?"

Eddie stood up and stretched his back. "It's a bit achey like." He held his right elbow guiltily; "I been using it a bit already."

98

Standback picked up a couple of stones and started his next row. "Didden mean to take so long," he said.

"Go down the cove?"

"Did as it happens."

"Mother used to say path only fit for goats," Eddie paused. "Sit in that seat and watch the seals did you?

Standback stared at his brother.

"You allus did that when we was kids, when you had the black dog on you," said Eddie.

"How'd you knaw?"

"Followed you once. Saw you sittin' down there lookin' at the seals."

"I never saw you."

"Didden want you to. Was your secret. You not knowin' that I knew, that was my secret. Went down there myself sometimes, see what it was all about. Wanted to be like my big brother I s'pose." He felt the photo in his sling guiltily. "Never saw no seals though."

"They'll come, you call 'em," said Standback.

The photograph seemed to burn a hole in Eddie's shirt beneath his sling. Eddie finished tamping the fill and then he too began the next row. "Reckon we'll finish it tonight," he said.

The Tides of Life

The sound of the waves crashing over Cap'n Billy's pool was still in Standback's head. On the rocks it had calmed him, up here it made him restless. He watched Eddie working and wondered at his ability to carry on through everything. His brother obviously felt the chasm between them just as much as he did. They'd been dancing around it all day. He decided to try conciliation.

"Still out St. Just?" he asked.

Eddie nodded.

"How're the girls?"

"Jen an' Steve live up Bristol now. Got two kids, one at university. Tamsyn's a teacher, she live over Helston way."

"See 'em much?"

"Christmas. Sometimes 'ere and sometimes up at Jen an' Steve's. Course they all try get down home summer. Bit of a houseful then, with the grandkids an' all. Christine d'keep in touch. She do all the messaging an' stuff on computer, allus talk to the grandkids an' all like that."

"Don't you talk to 'em?"

"I got a phone, but mostly so Christine ring me. Can't get on with all that technology . . . You?"

"Did a course once at the library."

"You did?"

"Useful for gettin' jobs an' all."

"S'pose."

"You still down Geevor then?"

"Idden many of us left. Not many as actually worked down there afore it closed. I give talks an' that down there as well, an' talks on farming 'course."

They worked on in silence. Neither one of them was feeling satisfied with their brief discourse.

Atlantic Rollers

The wind was strengthening and the sea rattled the rocks in the cove. It swirled and boiled around Seal Island and sputtered and spat into Cap'n Billy's pool. The sea was teasy, building up to a storm; the pleasure boats cut short their final trips to the seals and turned for home. In St. Ives, the surfers parked up in the narrow strip of car park above Porthmeor Beach and left their jeeps and SUVs to ride the surf on their boards. The mussels tightened their grip on Mussel Point; and deep in Cap'n Billy's pool the crabs scuttled about as the waves shuffled the rocks, and the seals rolled around in the froth between the breakers. Off Hayle estuary, out towards Portreath, the Brixham schooner *Ebenezer* moaned as she rolled over on the ocean bed. Bound for Topsham with Newport coal she'd been wrecked during a NNW gale in February 1832. On the footpath above the long harbour wall behind the new Asda, the wooden wreck-carved statue of a woman holds aloft a fish and faces the sea to welcome the change of air. The great Atlantic rollers slap against the granite, slowly and interminably wearing away the cliffs. Whether the harvest be pilchard, tin or visitor, the everlasting clash of salty Atlantic roller and fiery granite cliff continues to play with life and death, continues the process of erosion and evolutionary change.

Strange is the Past - i

Eddie had changed. This morning he'd had something on his mind but he'd been cocky. Now he was still hiding something, but he wasn't so cocky. He was less easy somehow. Standback watched him. Eddie was too quiet and he wouldn't meet his brother's eyes. He wondered what it was that had changed while he'd been down at the cove. He was more than ever sure that Eddie was hiding something, or building up to say something. One thing was certain, whatever he imagined it might be, it wouldn't be. Since they'd been kids, Eddie had always managed to get upset by the last thing he could imagine, like the time he'd broken Eddie's bow. It had been a birthday present, a plastic bow and a set of three arrows with rubber stops. Eddie had found a picture of it in a catalogue and had gone on and on about how much he wanted it. He'd been so excited on the morning of his birthday and he'd gone out with Father to shoot at the barn while Standback was sent to hose down the yard. Later in the day Standback had found the bow on the hay bales and had picked it up. Then he took it outside and had taken aim at a tin can he'd balanced on a fence post, like he'd seen in the cowboy films. He'd pulled back on the string to make the arrow zing and the plastic bow snapped. He'd put it back where Eddie had left it and said nothing. He'd felt sick with worry because Eddie would be upset and then his parents would be angry with the big brother who should know better; but Eddie didn't care. He came in from the fields with a new bow which he'd made with string and a sycamore branch; and when Father'd asked what had happened to the birthday present, he just said, "It was only a toy. This one's real." It was the very last thing Standback had expected his brother to say. Father had moaned about the cost of the present, but otherwise nothing was ever said about the plastic bow being broken.

He stood up and took off his cap to wipe his brow. Eddie was working fast despite his arm.

"Any more tea in that flask?" Standback asked.

Eddie didn't stop working; "Help yourself. Be a bit cold."

Standback picked up the flask and poured himself some tea. He shook the flask. "'Nuff for two. Fancy one?"

Eddie shook his head without looking up.

"Been using that arm a lot more as the day go on," said Standback. "Father allus say you improve an injury by working through it."

Eddie nodded. "Stiffen up else he used to say."

Standback leaned back against the hedge. "I been thinking about the past," he said.

102

Eddie stared at him. "How d'you mean?"

"Strange how the past idden the way you remember it," said Standback.

"How?"

"I allus felt guilty I missed Jack's funeral."

Eddie looked non-plussed. "But you was there."

"I wadden really. I was drunk. See life don't go in straight lines. Last year, this year, next year, thass a line. People talk about the past like that don't they? A timeline or lineage, a family line . . ."

Eddie was looking distinctly uncomfortable.

"Well. They're wrong see. Life go in waves, forrard an' back at the same time. Big things happen . . . like the crest of a wave breaking, but then they swirlin' an' boilin' around like the water between the waves, so that one big thing is part of the next big thing an' the last big thing all to once!"

He'd surprised himself by being able to describe what he'd discovered down in the cove.

"You been drinking?" Eddie asked.

The Hospital

His father had seemed to shrink in the clean and clinical waiting room of Treliske Hospital. He suddenly seemed much older, an old man, no longer the tall broad-shouldered man who'd dragged him into the barn to wrestle. He hadn't noticed before quite how much weight his father had lost. His best jacket seemed a size too big. They'd chatted in the car on the way to Truro but not about much. It had been mostly Standback trying to make conversation. He'd talked about the increased traffic, the impatience of other drivers, but he could hardly get a word out of his father. He supposed that he hadn't tried as hard as he might because all he'd really wanted to talk about had been the farm; and the same old argument about how he felt betrayed by the sale of the cliff fields to the National Trust. It should have been Eddie who'd driven their father to Truro, Eddie could have made everything feel better. His father would have preferred Eddie. What was it he'd said? Just one small comment. They'd had to brake as a car came out in front of them without indicating. One small thing he'd said. "Eddie do allus take it slow when the trippers are out." It was the way they were. His father hadn't actually accused him of bad driving, he hadn't been angry with the driver who had come out in front of them without indicating, he'd merely suggested that it wouldn't have happened if Eddie had been driving. But of course Eddie wasn't living on the farm. Eddie had to work, take the kids somewhere, pick Christine up. Eddie had his own life. Whereas Standback's life had still been on the farm, or what was left of it, so he'd been the one to drive their father to hospital.

A brisk young nurse called out "Mr Hosken!" His father held his hand up. It struck him as funny, his father behaving like a kid in school. He'd never seen his father subservient. The nurse smiled and came over to them.

"This way, Mr Hosken." She took his father's arm as he stood up and he didn't stop her. When they'd arrived at the hospital, Standback had tried to help his father out of the car but his father had pushed him away irritably. "I'm not an invalid!" he'd said.

Standback hadn't known what to do.

"Is this your son?" the nurse asked his father. His father nodded.

"Thought so," she said, "dead spit of you, Mr Hosken." She flashed a smile over his father's head. "It's always good to have

104

company isn't it?" Then she looked at her notes. "You've come a long way. I expect the roads were busy."

Standback nodded. "Yes," he said.

"Not too bad at all," said his father.

The nurse flashed Standback another smile. "I was held up half an hour at Chiverton roundabout this morning," she said.

They were ushered into a side room to wait for the doctor. It was small and white with blinds over the window. There was a patient couch covered with a long sheet of disposable paper, a blue screen was pulled back at the foot of the couch. There was a sink in one corner, with a soap dispenser for hand washing and paper towels; and two plastic chairs in front of a radiator.

"Doctor will be with you shortly," said the nurse and left them, father and son, awkwardly side by side on the orange plastic chairs, staring out through the open door into the busy corridor. He hated the harsh bright interior lighting and turned to peek out through the blinds, hoping to see sunlight and sky. All he could see was more white walls like a corridor in which someone had planted bamboos. Then he realised that it was a sort of outside corridor and that they were the same bamboos that he'd seen through the big windows in the main waiting room. He felt sorry for the bamboos, imprisoned in the channel between the walls of two waiting rooms.

He couldn't remember much more, just the look on the doctor's face when he'd told his father that he had cancer and that it was terminal. He remembered having an image of a bus station as his brain went into denial. His father had been sitting bolt upright in the chair.

"How long have I got, Doctor? Months?" he'd asked.

"I can't give you a definitive answer, Mr Hosken, but I'd say that with care, and regular visits for transfusions, you might have four good years."

His father had looked so small, huddled in the passenger seat of the car on the way home.

Strange is the Past – ii

"Remember last time we got drunk together, Eddie?"

"Jack's funeral, up the North Inn."

"Father'd found out he had cancer week before."

Eddie looked surprised. "Did he? I thought it was after that."

"See what I mean!" said Standback. "Life don't happen in a list. It's all goin' on to once. Thass why it's so hard to remember. They said he had four years to live when I took him up the hospital. No one seemed to notice that, 'cept me. You were still doin' shift work down Geevor. Then there was Jack's funeral. We was all up the North Inn to remember Jack; but all I could think of was the doctor's face when he'd told us, Father an' me, that Father had cancer. An' how small Father looked huddled down in the passenger seat of the car on the way home from Truro. That trip was the first time he never drove hisself."

"I remember him tellin' us but I didden knaw it was then."

"Was tea time. A week before Jack's funeral. He'd got a grip of hisself by the time we got home an' it didden seem so serious when he said it. He didden even look so ill at home. Not like when he was sittin' on that plastic chair in the waitin' room at the hospital. 'They reckon I got four years,' he said."

"But like Mother say," Eddie said, "no one knew for sure, 'cos new cancer drugs bein' found every day."

"An' he let her think it. Let us all think it. I went up Bristol thinkin' it. Everyone was trying to act as though everythin' was normal. I coulden get that picture of him out my head though, the little small thin man in the big plastic chair. Thass all I could think of Jack's funeral. I drank whole bottle of whisky to drown it . . . coulden . . . coulden do it. Coulden think of Jack; only the little thin man in the hospital. I was drinkin' for Father and he wasen even dead yet, but I felt like he was, d'you knaw what I mean?"

Eddie looked uncomfortable. "You . . . you was fixin' for a fight. I knaw that."

"I don't remember when I got so used to the fact that he was alive that I forgot he was dyin'."

"Like you say, you was drinkin' a lot back then, Standback. No wonder it all rolled into one."

The conversation wasn't going the way Standback had planned and now he was justifying himself. "I was bustin' a gut earn money for Trevarnon. He knew that an' all. An' he still got rid of they fields to the National Trust."

"He didden want to saddle the farm with debt."

"Woulden've been a problem if he'd let go, handed over to me. Why coulden he trust me? His own son?"

"You was fixin' for a fight I know that," said Eddie.

"I tried to talk to him Jack's funeral."

He found himself back in a place he'd found himself so often, he sank down against the hedge.

"Well come on Eddie. This is the time you tell me I was feckless, ran away, drank too much, useless, whatever."

"You didden. You didden drink too much."

Standback stared at his brother, Eddie was noticeably nervous. "What? What is it?"

"What's what?"

"You're hiding something."

"What you on about?"

Standback's eyes were steely . . . "I knaw you, Eddie. What is it? You can't fool me. I knaw that arm idden so bad as you let on."

Eddie touched his sling involuntarily.

Standback stared. "What you got in there?"

Eddie stepped back. "Nuthen."

"You got somethin' hidden in your sling."

"I haven't." Eddie found himself pinned against the hedge.

"Bleddy liar! What is a?"

Standback grabbed hold of his brother's arm. Eddie didn't even wince, but he looked terrified.

"All right," he said, "all right, juss remember you made me show it." He reached into the sling and pulled out the photograph.

Standback snatched it. "It's Jack! Jack and ... an' ... Mother ..." Turning the photograph over, he read the back, "Yes, Jack and Mother, Synku Mój. . ." The smell of the interior of the little tin hut wafted over him, the paraffin and oil Jack rubbed into the wood mixed with the warmth of the little stove and the musky scent of the young vixen. "Synku mój . . . my son . . . Jack never had no son." Even as he turned the photo over he felt light-headed and his heart seemed to jump beneath his tee shirt. "Thass mother, an' Jack . . . with a . . . a baby?" He stared at his brother; "Where'd you get this?"

Eddie was silent, Standback caught hold of his brother's jacket and held the photograph up to his face. "Where'd you get this?"

"Don't mean nuthen," Eddie said.

Standback held the photograph hard up against Eddie's nose. "Where'd you get this?" he repeated.

"You're hurting my bad arm," said Eddie.

"You idden so hurt, Eddie. Think I haven't watched you work?"

For a moment they stared into each other's eyes. Eddie looked away first, staring at the pile of earth he'd scuffed over the wooden box in the fill where he'd been working. "I found it, in that old box there," he said, "over in the fill."

Standback followed his brother's gaze. He went to the fill and brushed off the loose soil. "Uncle Jack's box!" He went to pick it up. "Tes too, Uncle Jack's box. He said it held his life history."

"Don't mean nuthen," said Eddie.

"I haven't seen this since that night, the night in the hut." He held the carved box, gently brushing earth from the faded carving. "Look, you can still see the birds and flowers, after all these years." He ran his fingers over the lid. He felt sick. His heart felt as if it was turning cartwheels beneath his ribs. He opened the box. Slowly he lifted out some paper, it was folded and cut out into holes. Very very gently he prised apart the folds, until the frail paper fell open to reveal the most intricate and beautiful wycinanka cut-out.

"The war does strange things to people," he said. "I been told that twice. All these years I thought it had somethin' to do with money!" He laughed. "Can you believe it!" His hands shook as he placed the box on the ground. He sunk his head into his hands. "Your father's box," she said. "Your father's box. The war does strange things to people."

Eddie was dumbstruck as the sense of what his brother was saying rested upon him. It didn't really change anything, in fact it made things worse. Their father had always favoured his big brother. This would be yet another excuse for Standback to be dark and belligerent, for his brother to be outside of things, for his filling all the space in their father's love for his sons, so that Eddie always knew he was the second best. He spoke the end of his thoughts out loud, "And the mighty first-born's really a bastard!" He laughed.

"You knew! You've known all along!" Standback took a step towards Eddie.

"Don't be so bleddy stupid. I'm the sad bastard that's lived all his life in the shadow of a brother who didn't exist! Got to laugh at that haven't you!"

"You knew an' you said nuthen!"

The Challenge

Eddie was scared and angry. "I 'aven't never seen that picture before."

"Liar! You got me up 'ere do this job, an' you put this 'ere for me to find."

"Course I didden."

"You set me up. All that talk about finding things in hedges." He walked towards Eddie.

"I didden. I juss found it. Look at it! That box been buried years."

Standback hadn't planned to do it. It just happened, just as it had sometimes when they were kids rolling around the barn floor when they'd had a fight. Eddie recoiled as his brother's fist punched him hard in the stomach.

"I didden knaw nuthen 'bout it," spluttered Eddie. "An' thass the God's honest truth."

"Think I don't knaw when you're lyin', little brother. You got me up here on purpose!" Standback crouched, fists clenched for the fight. He began to circle his brother.

"Alright, alright! Yes, I got you up 'ere! I did! But I 'aven't never seen that photograph, never in my life. I got you up 'ere because I wanted to beat you like I beat John Matthews!"

Standback stood stock still and stared at his little brother. Then he laughed out loud.

"What the hell you sayin'! You! You beat John Matthews!"

"Never even crossed your mind did it? Never crossed your

110

mind I could beat John. I hurt my arm doin' it an' all, but I beat him, an' then I knew I could beat you. But I had to get you down 'ere first. All my life, Standback! All my life I've lived under your shadow!"

The Winner

It had felt so good. Everyone was cheering, all his friends, the whole pub. John Matthews had been gracious in his defeat, he'd bought a round for everyone and toasted the new winner, *"Eddie Hosken!"* he shouted and the pub roared it back: *"Eddie Hosken!"*

Then there'd been another toast, and another, *'Eddie Hosken!'* Everyone loved to see the underdog come through to win. The pub had been ringing with song. Beers kept coming and he'd felt taller than he'd felt in his whole life. Eddie had felt like a king.

John had been the one to mention it first. "I been beaten by both Hosken boys now. Knaw what that d'mean?"

They were on the whisky, never Eddie's favourite drink. He couldn't hold it together like John or his brother. Of course he could've if he'd had the chance, wasn't his fault. Christine's father'd had a taste for the Golden Lady and Christine had put her foot down, but tonight he threw caution to the wind. John had mentioned having seen Standback in Penzance. "Come down for Billy's funeral," he'd said.

He remembered he'd joked with John about his brother and Billy being two of a kind, wild boys who thought they could live on the outside, different from everyone else. They'd laughed a lot and the rounds kept coming. "Question is," said John, "which of you boys is best? Thass what I d'want to knaw." He paused to let it sink in. "You 'aven't got much time," he'd said, "Standback's goin' back up Bristol day after tomorrow."

111

John's words swam around his head here at Dry Stone Hedge, just as they had in the pub, and so did his answer to John.

"I told him. 'John,' I said, 'you get my brother up 'ere, get him up Trevarnon, up where I'm workin'. He won't come for me, but he'll come for you, an' he'll come for Trevarnon.' Thass right though idden'a, Standback? You come up 'ere for John, you come up for the farm! You woulden of come up for me."

Eddie got to his feet and crouched. "C'mon, you're fixin' for a fight, I'll give you one!"

Standback stared at his little brother. "This idden about you Eddie!"

Eddie watched as Standback turned to walk away from him, up towards the copse.

"No, it's always about you, isn't it? Isn't it, Standback! Everythin's allus about you! All my life it's allus been about you!"

But Eddie was shouting into the empty air.

The Roots go Deep

Eddie had always wanted to be like Standback. His brother was confident, strident, his brother knew he was right. Eddie wasn't certain about himself. He wanted to be confident, he wanted to know exactly who he was and what he thought; and he wanted not to have to suffer the confusion of the many opinions he considered. He wanted to know what it was like to know he was right.

Standback thought Billy Blewett was some sort of hero because he'd hidden in the corner of a field with his ducks and his ferrets. Eddie knew the reality, Billy wasn't no better than old Happy Harry, the tramp who'd walked the lanes back in

112

Grandad's day: or the New Age Travellers who'd built the benders down Kenidjack Quarry. Some people had admired the travellers' attempt to live a simple life; others thought they should be cleared out like vermin. The 1994 Act made Civil Trespass a criminal offence and the bulldozers went in. Billy thought he was living the old life but he was only feeding the new. He capered for the new owners of his dad's farm. How could Billy and Standback believe that camping out on that splatt of land somehow made Billy triumphant, as though he'd got something over on the new owners? That's how Standback saw it but it made no sense to Eddie. Couldn't Billy see he was still being used? Just a colourful local. Couldn't he see that he was capering to the incomers? It was all too muddled up for Eddie. Eddie liked clarity. Still, there was some justice in getting top price off the second home owners for vegetables grown on their own land.

Deep deep down in his roots, Eddie felt betrayed. He'd always done the sensible thing. He'd worked just enough at school to get by. He'd known the farm was there to support him, but as he came of age he could see that Trevarnon could not keep them all. He'd met Christine at The Barn Club in Penzance and fallen in love straight away. Christine had a Saturday job at Tesco and earned more than he did working on Saturday and every evening milking on the farm. Christine's father and her two elder brothers and cousin were all miners; the family lived in Pendeen. Miners were on good money in the seventies, Christine's mum had the latest washing machine, bathroom, fridge. Her brother had a Cortina. They had spending money in their pockets. Eddie had felt ashamed to park the farm's old Land-Rover outside the *Trewellard Arms*. He started to spend a lot of time in Pendeen. Christine came to Trevarnon Farm only once. In her suede platform shoes and maxi-skirt she delicately crossed the muddy yard. She was the jewel he wanted to show off to his parents. They'd had a cream tea which Christine couldn't eat because she was 'watching her weight' and it had seemed to Eddie that everything in the farmhouse kitchen seemed old and inadequate by comparison to Christine's mother's shiny Formica kitchen. It was dark when Christine left and despite the yard light, she was unable avoid stepping in the mud and her maxi-skirt from *'Chelsea Clobber'* in St. Ives trailed in the foul-smelling liquid. When she got home she threw the suede platforms and the maxi-skirt into the bin. She didn't visit the farm again and Eddie never pressed her on the point. A few months later he signed on at Geevor and by the end of the year, with a little help from both sets of parents, Christine and Eddie were married at Penzance Registry Office and moved into their own cottage in St. Just. Rented for a year, but they'd soon managed to get a first mortgage. Funny really, back then a Land-Rover wasn't very sexy; now everyone wanted four wheel drives and Land-Rovers.

He'd enjoyed working at Geevor Tin Mine. The camaraderie suited him. It was hard and heavy work, not to mention dangerous, but he was proud to be a miner. He'd still done the hedging and he and Christine managed well. But despite his financial and social success Eddie had always felt like second best: even after Standback went to Bristol. His elder brother had returned twice and been received as the prodigal son. Eddie never understood why they welcomed him home so readily. At the same time he felt too ashamed to invite Christine round to Trevarnon Farm a second time. He imagined that her family saw him as a country clod. He concentrated on his new job and when the price of tin fell, Eddie wanted, more than anything else, to believe the words he had heard in David Penhaligon's speech in Camborne in 1986.

114

Deckchairs & Ice Cream

On Friday 28th November 1980 the Queen opened a new shaft at Geevor Tin Mine. It was called Victory Shaft, a brave and successful name. They'd actually started digging Victory in 1919. In 1975 they decided to drive a sub-incline shaft from Victory to connect the eighteenth level with lower submarine levels at Levant Mine. The extension was completed in 1979. Queen Elizabeth II, in her white miner's hat and a white coat and white boots actually walked into the mine, went down to Level 15, 1800 feet. They'd had a great night up the pub after that. Things were going to be all right.

Geevor, like everywhere, had been affected by the power cuts of the early seventies. They'd had to cut consumption of electricity. It had been worse for the farms though. The power cuts were done on a time rota, but cows need to be milked at the same time every day. Then there were the dairies. The milk lorries often had to wait or come back later. Coal stocks were dwindling and the local newspaper, *The Cornishman,* announced that Hayle Power Station might have to stop running altogether. But Geevor survived all of that and in 1980 the sight of Queen Elizabeth II in her white miner's hat and white coat and boots, and the official opening of Victory felt as if they had won the battle of power cuts, and despite the falling price of tin they could look forward to a good future. Geevor would go on, no danger, because the Queen had come down to open Victory. Nobody believed that Geevor Mine would close, everyone clung on to the belief that something would happen.

Five hundred people, including Eddie, Christine and the girls, went up to London with Ray Rodden and Mick McArdle, and other members of the Transport & General Workers'

Union; and Eddie's boss Ken Gilbert, the Miners' wives support group, and Pendeen Silver Band. They went to make the case for Geevor Mine. They also went to Camborne to listen to their local MP, David Penhaligon in 1986, fifteen hundred people gathered. The girls hadn't really understood but Christine and Eddie were sure that the politicians in London must listen after that speech. Eddie remembered every word. Sometimes he told the visitors when he showed them around Geevor: "You need more in an economy than just tourism, ice cream and deck-chairs," he'd say, repeating the famous words from David Penhaligon's address. Most people didn't really hear him, they were thinking about getting into the cafe for lunch before the queues. "We asked for a loan of 20 million, that's all." Eddie had to admit that the politicians had used him, same as the new owners of Carn Farm had used Billy. "I can see all the work you men are doing," said the man from the Department for Trade and Industry, "I can see no reason why the Government shouldn't invest in your mine."

Two months later it was Black Friday. Eddie's shift was underground when the news was announced. There would be no government loan. The miners had kept to their side of the bargain; their promise to work a nine hour day for eight hours pay in order to pay back a loan. Then they'd come up to find the press waiting. "How d'you feel about the mine shutting?" Microphones and cameras flashing. Even then no one could believe that Geevor would close.

'276 to lose jobs in Geevor Shutdown' was the headline in *The Cornishman* on Thursday April 3rd 1986. Mr Gilbert had addressed the miners. The total workforce had been some 375 and there would be men kept on for maintenance, but 276 had to collect all their personal possessions from the mine and finish work. Mr Gilbert would continue the appeal for government aid to keep the mine going. Everybody hung on to the belief that something would happen.

Something did eventually happen; the man from the Department for Trade and Industry hadn't lied, not exactly. There was investment. An investment of thirty million pounds would be found to turn Cornwall's mining remains into a Tourism Centre, A World Heritage Area. Eddie had another job now, as a guide he showed the tourists around a major heritage attraction. He was proud to be able to talk about the grizzly, proud to talk about stope holes, air-legs, trammers, calciterite; but inside he hurt, he hurt so badly. He and Christine had been lucky, they owned their cottage; other mining families had found themselves facing eviction when the new directors of Geevor Mine gave the tenants of eight mine-owned cottages at Trewellard notice to quit. British Rail had done the same with houses at Chy-an-Mor. Eventually the local district council bought the houses. It hadn't helped Eddie's friend Willy John who'd moved up country to work in coal mines and never came home. As Eddie saw it proud ordinary hard-working people had been used. He tried to make up for it as he told the visitors about hard-rock mining. People were happy to hear about the distant past, bal maidens, knockers, some even wanted pasty recipes. They wanted the romance of a hard life on the North Cornish coast as they'd seen it on TV dramas and the picture postcards they sent home to friends. They didn't want the romance to be sullied by the story of Willy John's family breaking up, of Willy John having to go up north to work in coal. Eddie continued with his talks about hedging. The Old Cornwall Society audiences listened to the whole of David Penhaligon's speech and they always cheered and clapped; at the University of the Third Age, their members would nod sagely; and in the depths of his being, Eddie just felt betrayed.

Some things should Stay Buried

Things found in Cornish hedges were one of the favourite topics at Eddie's talks. It made a good finish to a talk. He had two boxes of 'finds'. He'd never understood why people were so fascinated by the detritus of others. They wouldn't go through their neighbour's wheelie-bins with the enthusiasm they demonstrated as they dug into his box of 'finds'. They loved the old blue poison bottles, the bits of crock, the flints, the old knives, and coins. The one they liked best was the story of the skeleton of a baby. He couldn't actually remember where he'd first heard the story himself, or even whether it was true, but it was not impossible. Where else could a starving family bury a still-born child? He assumed it was one of Grandad's stories. He also told his audiences how people sometimes buried a crock in the cool side of a hedge in which to keep butter chilled. Then, he'd open the other box, this one held the plastic that he sometimes found entangled in the blackthorn, where it trapped birds and insects; and the cans tossed out of car windows, in which creatures could be trapped: and the sandwich cartons, he'd even found used nappies. Then he'd show the foreign cigarette packets, names in Polish or Lithuanian. Modern day detritus tells another story, he'd say. Once he'd found an old Oxo tin in which there was a pack of cards, a dinky toy car, and a picture of a teddy bear on which it said 'Growler', and a note written in young handwriting. It said, 'I Peter Quick, aged 9, have buried this time capsule in 1976'.

But Eddie wished he hadn't found the box with the carved top.

Something Changed in the 1970s – ii

Farming became 'intensified'. If you intensify a taste, it's better and stronger. The Dictionary definition of the adjective would be 'concentrated, intense, strained, unremitting'. In agricultural terms it is 'obtaining the maximum yield from the soil of a limited area.' The motivation is profit and to rid the world of hunger. In order to create more food for the world and to be competitive with price, hedges were pulled down, the fields were enlarged, machinery became bigger, insecticides became more powerful. As these changes happened, farming became less labour-intensive and more reliant upon machines. There were still times when extra labour was needed, for planting and picking. Arduous and repetitive work which could be done cheaply by the populations of the countries with a poorer economy than the United Kingdom. The local crews found themselves undercut and saw no reason for working for such low wages. Equally, the biggest landowners grew richer as they saw the opportunity to buy cheap agricultural land in Eastern Europe. Nobody realised how damaging the overall effect of such changes in farming might be to the land, the very soil of the earth itself, and the diversity of life which relied upon its balance.

A global world has a great many benefits. It should engender peace and an understanding of difference; but in the chase for profit and the innate greed and need for power and control which singles out the human animal, it seems only to exaggerate difference and to encourage defensiveness, borders and divides. Some argue that Man only developed these traits when he stopped hunter-gathering and began to grow crops and to keep animals, necessitating the need to claim property of the land

and to build fences to protect his crops and beasts. Eddie had often thought that if the world could be managed in the same way as the Cornish hedges, there might be some sort of harmony of existence. However he also watched the birds and saw the pecking order. They existed, foraged, fed, fought off enemies, flew to escape predators and did these things because living was what they had to do. It was the same with people.

The world became global and somehow the world seemed smaller. It became easier to travel to other places. The supermarkets filled with fruits and vegetables regardless of season; it was always a growing season somewhere and suddenly everything was available to all, all year round.

The bumblebee on the thistle, the lizard sunbathing on the stony dust, the robin singing low in the gorse, the blackbird singing from the hawthorn, the rabbit in his burrow, the hedgehog and the fox and the orange-tip butterfly and hummingbird hawk moth knew nothing of this. While man expanded his horizons, his fields, his sales, his appetites, over two thirds of the species whose kingdom had been the Cornish hedges were eliminated by the flail. This new cutting implement turned blackthorn and gorse to mush, destroyed nests and caterpillars. The mulching effect left by the flail formed barriers to the small plants and allowed the stronger, invasive hogweed, bracken and bramble to take over. No one considered the decline in the harvest within the Cornish hedges until too late.

Some people were beginning to realise. This was why set-aside land had been so important. The Guild of Cornish Hedgers published evidence of the loss of species and outlined the causes. The hedges were being flailed at the wrong time of year, just when the birds were nesting, and often on both sides. 'There is a better mechanical tool, the reciprocating scythe, the finger-bar cutter', said the Guild. 'This is the tool which should be used,' said the Guild, 'and the cutting should be done in late winter, and alternative sides of the hedge should be cut in different years.'

The Guild of Cornish Hedgers have leaflets about every aspect of Cornish hedges.

"Everyone have his own way"

Eddie had been asked along to Zennor Village Hall. The University of the Third Age was hosting a talk by the Guild of Cornish Hedgers and somebody had suggested inviting the Hosken Boys. Only Standback lived up Bristol so Eddie alone had attended as a practising hedger. He had felt uncomfortable. The audience was made up mostly from new residents to the area, people from the cities and middle England who were keen to feel at home in the granite land, and who wanted to become involved in local cultural activities.

Afterwards, Eddie had thought to himself, "Wadden wrong exactly, what he said. I mean he gave the facts an' all but how can he know it for real, if he hadden lived it? Someone have to tell him."

Eddie had felt shut in at the village hall. It was hot, the tea was weak, and they'd had pasties with basil and feta cheese.

Eddie could never have done it unless he'd been invited. In his mind the meeting was really nothing to do with him. He was not a part of it, and was only there because someone had said you want to get the Hosken Boys along. He'd been wondering how to leave from the moment he entered the hall, and wished he'd stayed at the back of the room, rather than going down to the front row as invited. His name had been written down on a piece of paper on a plastic chair. His surname had been spelled Hosk*ing* instead of Hosk*en*. It had annoyed him.

"So, before we bring tonight to a close," the Chairwoman

121

f

was standing, "perhaps we might hear from a true Cornish hedger." She stared over her glasses along the front row.

Eddie Hosken sat like a frightened rabbit in the lamp-light. Minutes seemed to pass and the chairwoman nodded briskly towards him. "Mr Hosk*ing*?" she said brightly.

Eddie stood up slowly. "Well, I was taught by my father, and he was taught by his father. Thass the kind of trade he is . . ." His mouth felt dry and he wanted to run from the hall, then he heard himself say: "The thing about hedging is . . ." He paused. "Fact is, there's a right way, a wrong way, an' everyone have his own way."

He couldn't think what else to say. There was a hush in the hall. At that moment the screens to the kitchen rattled loudly as they were drawn open.

"Ah, the teas!" said the Chairwoman. "Perhaps next time you might tell us some more from your own unique perspective, Mr Hosking," she said.

"Hos*ken*!" said Eddie, surprising himself with his vehemence. The Chairwoman looked bemused. "Our name is Hosk*en*, not Hosk*ing*!"

The Chairwoman coughed. "It's only left for me to say thank you to the Guild for explaining the mysteries of Cornish hedging . . . and thank you to," she gave a look as if to say, how does it matter how I say his name, "to Mr Eddie," she drew a breath, "Hosk*en* . . . for coming along today."

Outside the hall, the speaker from the Guild caught up with Eddie. "I'm sorry if I came over as a little patronising. I didn't mean to be. My father hedged and I've been all over the county talking to the old boys, the boys my father knew, trying to get the knowledge written down to pass on. What people really need to hear is the story from an actual hedger. I had no idea you were here. I do hope you might come along to another meeting."

Eddie had been reluctant to accept the offer. As a hedger all his life, he knew there had been changes but he worried that the trade might be lost by becoming a hobby-craft undertaken in the same way as people tried out pottery, weaving and silver-smithing, only to give up eventually. Hedging was not just a job, to Eddie it was as much a way of life as it was to his brother, and a necessary activity in the care of the land. He'd listened as the speaker had talked about the methods of building a hedge. He had thought about it all, long and deep, as he listened to what was said. The Guild had amalgamated the ways of many of the old hedgers to make a template by which to train new hedgers.

Eddie accepted that farming had changed, he had understood that Trevarnon could not continue as it had done for years. He could see the evidence all around him; and, unlike Standback, he could see that his father had no choice but to capitalise on the offer from the National Trust. Many Cornish families had found themselves becoming forced to sell up in order to survive; not for profit. He'd understood that it had also made sense to sell the buildings of the farm. They went one at a time; the stone barn, the old mowhay, then the house. They became Trevarnon Barn, Trevarnon Studio, Trevarnon Old Farm House. New addresses for the place he had been brought up in as Trevarnon Farm. By then he was working at Geevor and shopping at the supermarket. He and Christine had been able to buy furniture on hire purchase, as advertised on their new colour rental television. Then, when Geevor finally closed, Eddie began to realise that it was all part of the same thing. That was when he had returned to the Guild to learn more, so that he could incorporate their knowledge with his own life knowledge and experience when he himself spoke about farming and the craft of Cornish hedging. After all, if a thing was going to be talked about, 'better fit the talker knaw his subject', as Grandad would have put it, and Eddie knew his subject.

Every Stone a Hole and Every Hole a Stone

Eddie's bid for ascendancy was going badly wrong. All his life he'd only wanted to stand side by side with Standback as an equal. He'd lived in his brother's shadow for all these years but now he didn't have a brother and, like a hedge with shiners – stones set in such a way that the framework of the hedge was unstable – his whole life was falling apart. It was bloody typical of his brother. Standback could make you believe black was white if he wanted; like the beanstalk.

When Eddie had been seven years old, Standback had told him that if he planted a bean in a flower pot, it would be a foot high the very next day when he woke up, just like the bean stalk in the pantomime they'd been to see in Redruth. So Eddie had planted his bean in a flowerpot and finally gone to sleep. The following morning the plant was six inches high and there was a silver sixpence sticking out of the soil. He never questioned his brother, he asked for another bean and Standback had just said, 'the magic only works once'. It was years before he realised that his brother had simply exchanged the pot with the single bean for one of Grandad's stronger seedlings.

When he did find out he'd been upset because he felt foolish, but in later life, when he remembered it, he felt strangely pleased that his brother had bothered to make the magic happen for him. That was Standback, complicated, dark, confident, aggravating, and a contradiction. He knew all of that because he'd known his brother all his life.

Fibrous Roots

The sun was low but there was still light enough left in the day for Eddie to finish the top course. He pulled off the sling. He had planned the great revelation that his arm was recovered but the time had never seemed right. Now the time had passed. Things were different, there was no longer a plan, and there was little point in hampering himself. He threw the sling across the carved box, as though by doing so the box might disappear, together with its contents. If he hid it he could forget it existed. Perhaps that was why it had been buried in the first place. "What the eye can't see," His brother used to say to comfort him. It never did comfort him though. Just because he couldn't see something, it couldn't stop pictures coming into his head. He wished he could be like his brother, he wished he could show his emotions, 'let it fly' the way Standback could. He wished he didn't hide his feelings, he wished his mouth knew the way to speak the confusion of thoughts in his head. Standback just let it all out. Sometimes his brother didn't even make sense, sometimes he was wrong, and more often than not he would contradict himself. Then he would walk away, leaving Eddie tight, frustrated and afraid to speak. Standback could declare that he hated him one day and then deny it the next day; whereas Eddie believed in hatred, because he hated his own fears and inadequacies.

What Grandad said: *The Seeds of the Future*

Eddie began the tobbing off, the putting of turves on top of the hedge from which plants might grow. Roots were important, that was something he understood. As he loosened the matted fibrous roots he realised that they represented so many different plants. He couldn't tell one set of roots from another, except for tap roots. Tap roots should be good, they go deep and pure but Hogweed was not good in a hedge. It was the many shallow-rooted smaller plants, all melding together, which made the hedges into vertical meadows in the spring; which attracted the birds to nest and the butterflies and bees to drink.

Whether it was the fading light of the sun or the quiet as the birds began to roost he couldn't tell, but his grandfather's words seemed loud.

"Fibres... What we got 'ere, thass fibres, an' thass life, the continuum. What you can see in, over, an' beneath a hedge ... well, thass enough, full of life, full of stories ... if you knaw how to read 'em. Take the Wood Anemone, that survives from the time there was forests all over, it link us right back to then ... and Mexican fleabane. Miners brought that back. See, it's a circle, a continuum ... start with the granite an' life go on round it an' come back to it. Trouble is, he's happenin' too fast. Be alright if everyone could see the circle, see the Wood Anemone an' understand why it's there an' where it's come from. If everyone could read the hedges, the land, then they'd understand what's bein' saved, what's imported, an' what we're losin'. But you got to be able to read it. You got to knaw to understand. Got to read the land. Nowadays everyone's driven by money an' profit. We've forgot what we need juss for survival.

I never knew where I was goin' when I was a young man, but I knew where I'd come from an' I knaw it's okay to be where I am now. I feel it inside, it's what you feel inside. Idden no point in being resentful about people who don't understand. They have to be pitied for not having a place to be. I knaw I belong to be here."

Eddie turned abruptly but there was no one there. A blackbird uttered a warning cry from the hedge at the other end of the field, then all was quiet.

The Robin

The robin landed close to where Eddie was working. It turned its head cockily and eyed Eddie who stood perfectly still. The bird jabbed at the fresh earth and flew off with wings dripping from its mouth. Life and death in one movement.

He realised it was the first time it had come to him that day. For the last couple of days it had kept him company and he hadn't even noticed the little bird's absence. He felt guilty and reached into his pocket for a handful of mealworm that he'd taken from Christine's bird-food tin.

"Here go," he threw a handful down onto the hedge, just a little distant, and watched as the robin flew across to the food. Its left claw was damaged, causing it to limp. The bird turned its head to look down at the food, then back again to look at Eddie, then it filled its beak and flew back to the blackthorn to eat. Minutes later it was back for more. Eddie marvelled at the courage of the little bird, every day was a bonus. Even roosting must have been difficult with the injured claw. He'd watched the robin as it tried to balance on a telephone wire. It had flapped and wobbled and flapped but couldn't grip onto the wire, even with no wind to speak of. On the ground and on the thicker branches it could squat right down on its belly. Eddie knew that if it hadn't been for his feeding the bird, it might well not have survived. The nights had been cold, and even this early in the season the male birds were jostling for territory and mates. As he watched the robin fly in for food a third time, he saw that it wobbled as it leaned in to take the mealworm and it let down its left wing to lean on the ground like a crutch. It looked tired but it flew back to the blackthorn to eat. It carried on because there was no other choice, it had to eat, it had to sleep in a safe place at night, it had to mate, it was the only way to continue. It had to play its part. Eddie had seen the same thing in men. He couldn't imagine what his father had been through in the war, but he'd seen Matt Richards as he clawed at the grizzly before he fell. Matt hadn't been roped on. He would never forget the look in his fellow miner's eyes and the steel of the taut muscles that looked as though they might snap through his skin. He'd seen it on the farm too, the first time he'd shot a rabbit and it lay on the ground breathing desperately in a bid to stay alive. He'd learned then that everything is built to want to live. Even the fly in the spider's web hopes that by fighting the web it might escape. Eddie knew that the fighting was only part of dying; a body would fight to live and that was why he couldn't bare to sit with his mother, and had been glad that he hadn't had to drive his father to the hospital each month for blood transfusions. He had blocked it all out by concentrating on the new lives that he and Christine had brought into the world. He'd seen Matt Richards look death in the face and there had been nothing he could have done apart from bear witness; and he never wanted to be in that position again. However, as he watched the robin fly in for the last mealworm he smiled. It seemed to him that Standback was like that robin. He might be damaged, but his brother had the life force within him.

Down Black Water Side

"You could make me believe
with your lying tongue,
that the sun rose in the west."

When Standback started singing '*Down Black Water Side*' it usually meant that he was feeling guilty, it definitely meant that he was fighting drunk; but it also meant that the crisis was over.

Eddie looked over the hedge to watch his brother swagger down Longfield in the growing dusk, occasionally losing his footing. Eddie waited.

The Golden Lady

Standback held aloft a bottle of whisky which was almost two-thirds empty. "To Billy Blewett! Honest as the day is long!" His speech was slurred. He slithered to a stop, and held the bottle out to Eddie. "Will you drink with me? Drink to Billy Blewett!" Eddie shuffled.

Standback sank down against the hedge and laughed. "An' he allus have a drop of the Golden Lady stashed away down there."

"Down his field?"

"Ess, down Billy Blewett's land." Standback swallowed from the neck of the bottle and sighed, "Where is'a? Jack's box?"

"Under there." Eddie gestured to his sling on the pile of fill. Standback followed his brother's gaze; "Took it off then?"

"Gettin' in the way. I was hurt mind, I did need a sling for a while; juss wasen goin' to let on straight away that it was better."

Standback grinned. "John Matthews must've been mad as hell he lost to my little brother."

They stared at each other as though seeing each other for the first time. Standback passed the bottle to Eddie who took it. As he took a swig from the bottle he watched as his brother leaned across to drag the sling off the box. He watched as Standback gently took the box in his hands.

"Jack said his life was in this box," said Standback. "I seen it the night after Treveal Cliff. He showed me pictures of his mum an' dad, an' he had his mother's silver cross in it. Said he'd rather have had a fistful of memories."

Eddie took another pull at the bottle. He watched anxiously

as his brother opened the box and gently took out the wycinanka and laid it down carefully on the ground beside him. Then he lifted out the photograph and stared at it as if he'd never seen it before. Eventually he placed the photograph back in the box and reached across to Eddie, gesturing the bottle. Eddie passed it to him and watched as Standback took a deep draught. After drinking Standback stared at the level of the golden liquid, "Last quarter," he said. "Got to the level of reason," and passed the bottle back. He took up the wycinanka. This time he opened it completely. A folded piece of yellowing paper dropped out. Carefully, he laid down the intricate cut out, then picked up the yellowed paper and unfolded it with slow measured movements and read it. For some time he was silent, then he read it aloud.

"Dearest Jack. Yours in another lifetime, Mary." He paused. "Well, there it is." Eddie handed him the bottle. Standback finished off the whisky. "Belong to go back in the earth," he said.

Very slowly, he gently folded the note and the wycinanka and replaced them on top of the photograph in the box. Slowly, he stood up and buried the box into the hedge. Eddie watched. The sun was low in the sky and a damp mist was creeping up from the sea.

"Listen!" Standback said. "Hear that . . . You knaw the thing I miss most up Bristol? It's that sound of the sea on the rocks. You don't get that on the Channel. It's juss water. Lappin'. But down here . . . down here it's the Atlantic Ocean that's crashing against granite. He idden the same. I miss it."

Eddie stared at his brother.

"You alright?"

"I did run away," Standback said.

"I didden mean that," said Eddie.

130

"The night after we went Treveal cliff."

"You didden. I'd've known."

"No one knew, 'cept Jack. I packed my duffel bag an' went out two o'clock in the mornin'."

"How come I didden knaw?"

"Was a light in Jack's hut. That paraffin lamp he had? Jack was awake, he was nursin' the fox with the busted leg? He'd juss found her, that night. In one of Old Man Blewett's snares."

"Rocky . . . she used to sort of roll along when she was tiny? Kids at school thought he was crazy have a pet fox," said Eddie.

"Cześć," he says, likes'if was normal go visitin' the middle of the night. 'I'm leavin' I says, 'I hate it here an' I hate Father an' I'm goin' . . . 'Where you go?' He says. I say 'I'll work the waltzers with Jim Stevens.' . . . 'Then we must have drink to see you on your way,' he says, an' he pours two glasses of vodka . . . 'Polish vodka very good for thinking and this is very best vodka,' he said. 'Now, tell me all that has occurred with you'." He paused as he remembered.

"Thass how he spoke. Thass Jack!" Eddie remembered too. "Thass Jack, big words an' all. Were you really gonna work the fair?"

"I was. An' all the time I'm talkin', he's strokin' that fox cub, calmin' it, an he's calming me and that tin hut is all warm and full of that outside-inside sort of smell that was Jack. It felt safe, Eddie, an' he didn't say nuthen, juss listened to what I had to say. Then he put his arm round me and he said 'Synku Mój.' He said, 'Synku Mój, my son, you are lucky to have father.' That's when he told me about Warsaw an' seein' his father get shot, an' goin' to the camp up north in the ice, an' seein' his mother dyin' of starvation, an' eatin' the rats. Then he says to me, 'You must enjoy your father. You must give him a gift.' An' I didden knaw what to give him an' Jack says, 'Make him a wycinanka, a father would be pleased to have some luck made

131

for him by his son.' An' he helped me to make it too. Took ages cut out all they tiny little holes."

"Did you do it? Don't remember you ever givin' Father a doily. Did you give Father the doily?"

"Never had to. Dad woke me up six o'clock next mornin' go market. 'C'mon boy need your help with the new bull, two man job.' Him an' me was alright for a bit after that. Felt like he knew I'd come of age 'cos I'd stood up to him."

"I was bleddy furious when Mother tole me you'd gone market without me," Eddie said.

"Went up to see Jack again that night but he'd gone walkabout, took to the lanes soon after. I left the wycinanka on his table." He paused. "It's the one in that box."

The brothers sat in silence, each in his own thoughts until Standback spoke, "He was cut off from his roots, Eddie. How d'you cope with a thing like that? I've worked all over. Bristol, Southampton. Told myself I didden belong 'ere no more. Father gone, farm gone, Mother doolally, then she gone. Nuthen to keep me see? But I coulden stay away. It's still my country. I had to come back." He sighed. "I allus called him uncle . . . you never called him uncle. D'you think Mother told me call him uncle?"

It was wholly dark now, and they sat in silence; and the darkness drew them close.

Standback stared at him. "D'you think he knew? Father? I mean he wasted me. I coulden never do right, but I never felt he hated me."

"He loved the bones of you."

"But he could feel somethin', coulden he? Same as I did. An' Mother, she lived with that secret, all those years. No wonder she lost it at the end."

They sat in silence again.

132

"I'm bleddy starvin'," said Standback.

"I got a sandwich in my bag," said Eddie.

Standback laughed, "What 'aven't you got in that bleddy bag?"

The Other Half of the Sandwich

Eddie tore back the plastic cover of a pre-packed sandwich and handed it to his brother, "Which you want, Cheese & Pickle or Cheese & Tomato?" Eddie asked.

Standback laughed. "I've allus wondered who's got the other half," he said. "You knaw, when you get a sandwich in a selection pack . . ." He took a sandwich and stared at the pack before handing it back to Eddie. "I mean, normally when you share a sandwich, there's some sort of closeness. I could be sharing this with someone I don't knaw." He began to chuckle, "I s'pose I been doin' that all my life." He handed Eddie the other sandwich. "Til now. Now I knaw."

They ate in silence, then Standback blurted out, "He coulden help it!"

"Help what?" said Eddie.

Standback swallowed the last mouthful of sandwich. "It's true what they say about the Golden Lady, you have to drink your way down to reason." He stared at Eddie. "Father coulden help it. He didden knaw why . . . juss had to fight me every inch of the way . . . see!"

Eddie stared at his half of the sandwich.

"Idden you wantin' that, Eddie?"

Eddie shook his head and handed the sandwich to his brother. "I'd've given anythin' for him to care enough to fight me," Eddie said.

Normally Standback would have accused his brother of bringing things back to himself, but tonight he was full of reason and a surety he could not remember feeling since he'd been a boy. He stood up and rolled back his sleeves.

"Reckon you can best me then?" he asked.

Hands Across the Hedge

Eddie scrambled to his feet. "I've waited all my life for this," he said.

They stood either side of the newly-repaired hedge. Locking hands they began to wrestle. Standback couldn't remember the last time he had actually touched his brother. As he leaned in to hold his opponent's hand he realised that it felt comforting to feel Eddie's weight coming back at him. He was surprised at how strong Eddie was, not bad at all for a man who was no longer spending all his days in heavy work. It crossed his mind that he might let Eddie win but he couldn't resist pushing back. And then, as they locked eyes, Standback saw that he wouldn't have to try to let Eddie win.

Tangled Roots

Afterwards Eddie asked, "Do you feel diff'rant?"

Standback shook his head. "Do you?" he asked.

"I was thinkin' about roots . . . like you were saying," said Eddie, "an' what Grandad said about a hedge an' how when he put his hand into it when he was tobbin' off, how he said it was fibres, an' fibres . . . thass life, he said. An' all they roots, all they different plants jostling for space in one hedge," he paused as he thought. "Slobberjack went on become a councillor, an' she did a good job standin' up for folk. Her dad died in the mine . . . before I went there mind, long time afore. S'pose he must've

134

come here like Jack did. Never thought about it afore. She put down her roots 'ere see, she belong."

Standback nodded. They sat in silence for a while.

"I was scared," said Eddie. "Thass why I never wanted to sit with Mother. Anythin' to do with death see, but I dunno now. It's all one, isn't it? Life an' death. Soon as you're born you're dying. Grandad called it a continuum."

"Less go up the North Inn," said Standback.

Eddie nodded, "An' John Matthews buy the first round," he said.

What Grandad said about Continuum

"You can learn a lot from watching Nature, boy. You watch the plants an' that growin' an' dyin' back an' you'll see the secret of life is that you just gotta live. You gotta live, even if there's death all around you. See, without Death there idden no Life; but without Life . . . well, without Life there idden nuthen, nuthen at all."

The Hedge in Dry Field

The hedge in Dry Field had been standing proud for three thousand years. The moonlight glinted on the quartz crystals in the granite stones. Deep inside the granite, where no one could see, the crystals shone like diamonds. There was a warning cry from the blackbird hidden in the thicket of brambles in the copse as the owl flew low and swept up a vole in its talons. Low down in the old part of the hedge, down beneath the prickly gorse and blackthorn, the robin roosted; not far from the leafy covering where the hedgyboar had dug down to sleep out winter in a ball of spines. Close to the new repair, the rabbit saw there was no entry in the hard-tamped rab, not yet anyway. The fox and the badger marked the newly-repaired stones as they passed along, and the foxglove seed lay dormant in the soil, waiting to crack into life in warm spring sunshine.

The pub was warm and convivial when the Hosken boys walked in together.